"Using your ex... a new wife is one thing, but conducting the preliminary interview on th... met *and marri...* insensitivity. Y... and resources ... your heart des... Was it to rub my nose in it?"

When Elizabeth finally looked at Xander, he was staring at her with a look she couldn't interpret.

"I had a number of reasons."

She forced herself to remain poised. If he wanted to play mind games, he could play them on his own. She was here to do a job and nothing else. "Tell me what kind of woman you have in mind to marry."

Elizabeth waited for him to answer but his gaze remained on her, the same unfathomable expression on his gorgeous face.

Uncertainty crept up her spine. The way he was looking at her...

Xander took a mouthful of his drink and set the glass steadily on the table.

"I don't need you to find me a wife, Elizabeth. I already have one." He leaned forward and lowered his voice. "Our marriage was never annulled. We're still married."

Brides for Billionaires

Meet the world's ultimate unattainable men...

Four titans of industry and power,
Benjamin Carter, Dante Mancini, Zayn Al-Ghamdi
and Xander Trakas are in complete control
of every aspect of their exclusive world...
until one catastrophic article forces them
to take drastic action!

Now these gorgeous billionaires need one
thing—a willing woman on their arm and wearing
their ring! A woman falling at their feet is normal
but these bachelors need the *right* woman to
stand by their side. And for that they need the
Billionaire Matchmaker...Elizabeth Young.

This is the opportunity of a lifetime for Elizabeth,
so she *won't* turn down the challenge of finding
just the right match for these formidable tycoons.
But Elizabeth has a secret that could complicate
things for one of the bachelors...

Find out what happens in:

Married for the Tycoon's Empire
by Abby Green

Married for the Italian's Heir
by Rachael Thomas

Married for the Sheikh's Duty
by Tara Pammi

Married for the Greek's Convenience
by Michelle Smart

Available now!

Michelle Smart

MARRIED FOR THE GREEK'S CONVENIENCE

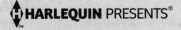

Recycling programs
for this product may
not exist in your area.

ISBN-13: 978-0-373-06032-0

Married for the Greek's Convenience

First North American Publication 2016

Copyright © 2016 by Harlequin Books S.A.

Special thanks and acknowledgment are given to Michelle Smart for her contribution to the Brides for Billionaires series.

Printed in U.S.A.

H HARLEQUIN®
™ www.Harlequin.com

Michelle Smart's love affair with books started when she was a baby, when she would cuddle them in her cot. A voracious reader of all genres, she found her love of romance established when she stumbled across her first Harlequin book at the age of twelve. She's been reading—and writing them—ever since. Michelle lives in Northamptonshire with her husband and two young smarties.

Books by Michelle Smart

Harlequin Presents

The Russian's Ultimatum
The Rings That Bind
The Perfect Cazorla Wife

One Night With Consequences

Claiming His Christmas Consequence

Wedlocked!

Wedded, Bedded, Betrayed

The Kalliakis Crown

Talos Claims His Virgin
Theseus Discovers His Heir
Helios Crowns His Mistress

Society Weddings

The Greek's Pregnant Bride

The Irresistible Sicilians

What a Sicilian Husband Wants
The Sicilian's Unexpected Duty
Taming the Notorious Sicilian

Visit Harlequin.com for more titles.

CHAPTER ONE

IF XANDER TRAKAS had thought his week couldn't get any worse, this was the nail in the coffin to finish him off.

His American lawyer, a thorough man if ever there was one, had confirmed that Xander's marriage to Elizabeth Young was indeed registered with all the relevant jurisdictions and authorities. However, there was no evidence of their annulment.

They were still married.

He grabbed the back of his neck and rubbed it hard, breathing deeply.

The whole *Celebrity Spy!* scandal was the mess that just kept giving. What had started as a relatively small teaser promising to reveal the 'juiciest and most scandalous details' about the world's most eligible and debauched bachelors had grown into the scandal of the decade. And to think he had dismissed that initial teaser... Yes, he was considered one of the world's most eligible bachelors, but debauched? He'd heard plenty of lewd stories about his new brothers in arms over the years. Compared to them he was practically a virgin.

Okay, that might be a notion too far, but a few monogamous affairs throughout the years had nothing on the legendary exploits of Dante Mancini, Benjamin Carter or Sheikh Zayn Al-Ghamdi.

The subsequent articles, not just in *Celebrity Spy!* but in its rival tabloids and websites the world over, had painted a picture of himself he simply did not recognise. Three of his ex-lovers had sold him out, embellishing and sensationalising what, to him, had been perfectly normal healthy affairs. Half a dozen women he struggled to remember even meeting had sold tales of their nights together. It was complete rubbish.

Strangely enough, the only woman from his past he hadn't worried about selling her soul for a piece of gold was the woman he'd made the mistake of marrying a decade ago.

All it needed was for one tenacious reporter to go digging through the court records and his marriage would be there for the world to see. It wouldn't take them long to put two and two together and see that while his jilted Greek fiancée had been falling apart at the seams, he'd been romancing and marrying an American beauty, oblivious to the destruction he'd left behind.

He'd never spoken of his marriage to Elizabeth. Not to anyone. Not his parents. Not his friends.

They'd never lived as man and wife. They'd met, married and gone their separate ways in a mad two-week period on the honeymooner's paradise of St Francis.

But their separate ways did not include the annulment Elizabeth had sworn—with an uncouth curse thrown at him for good measure—she would obtain.

The last time he'd seen her had been in their hotel villa. She'd had tears streaming down her shell-shocked face.

Did she know their annulment had been denied? Did the billionaire matchmaker know she was the legal wife of a billionaire herself? It beggared belief that she didn't know, but in all their years apart she'd never reached out to him, not once.

And he'd never reached out to her. He'd pushed her face from his mind almost completely.

He would have to tread carefully.

The report he'd had compiled on her had revealed a different woman from the one he'd known then. She was no longer a carefree nineteen-year-old who lived for nothing more than to feel the wind in her hair and the sun on her face. In the decade since they'd gone their separate ways she'd built a new and successful life for herself.

His phone vibrated, breaking through his thoughts. Hoping it would be his lawyer, who he'd ordered to find out exactly *why* their annulment had failed, he only just stopped himself pressing the accept button in time. The caller was his father, someone he was not in the mood to speak to.

Xander couldn't face another argument. The daily calls from Greece were becoming increasingly fractious, from both sides. Late last night, his sister-in-law had been admitted into hospital with alcohol poisoning. Liver failure had been diagnosed. Unless Xander's brother stopped shovelling drugs into his system, his body would be the next to break down.

All of this would have been difficult enough to cope with without having to deal with the major press intrusion the *Celebrity Spy!* scandal had unleashed.

Tonight he needed to keep himself together and his head straight. He would return home first thing in the morning but for now he had the annual gala for the Hope Foundation, the main charity he supported, to attend. The press would be out in force. All four of the men in the eye of the scandal would be under the same roof for the first time. They all supported this charity, and evidence was growing that it was now suffering because of its association with them.

Although their businesses lay in different fields, they'd been rivals for years. All four of them were strong, ultra-wealthy men with hard noses for business. There had been nothing friendly about their interactions. Tonight, he suspected they would have to find a way to breach their usual silent antagonism.

All four of them were feeling the pressure. They were in the eye of the storm and the sooner they found their way out of it, the better.

Two weeks later

Elizabeth Young stepped into her West Village apartment with a very real sense of relief. After a week away in Rome, she welcomed the return to the space she called home.

She loved her apartment, set in the heart of New York's oldest district. While it wasn't the largest piece of real estate around—she earned excellent money but not *that* excellent—she had never lived with such contentment anywhere else.

For perhaps the dozenth time since she'd landed at JFK, she checked her cell phone, telling herself it was concern for Piper that had her looking and not the looming possibility of her ex-husband getting in touch.

It was hearing Piper vocalise his name that had her so on edge. The beautiful Australian had been openly prying her with questions. Elizabeth didn't blame her. In Piper's shoes she would have been curious too. Three of the men implicated in the *Celebrity Spy!* scandal had called on her services so it was only natural the fourth would require her assistance too.

Dante did say Xander must call you too.

Were those Piper's words? They had definitely been something along those lines and had forced Elizabeth to confront what she had spent almost a fortnight in denial about.

Benjamin, Zayn and Dante had all said they'd been recommended to her by Xander. He'd passed her details to them.

She had no idea how her ex-husband knew what she did for a living or how he'd got her details. Leviathan Solutions was run in utter secrecy on a strict word-of-mouth basis.

She assured herself that just because he'd recommended her to the other men it didn't mean he required her services for himself. His situation was different from the others. Timos SE had been solely owned by the Trakas family for generations.

As a company, it owned countless beauty and clothing lines that were sold around the world. Their customer base couldn't care less about the scandal. They had no shareholders to pacify or stock markets to tumble from. Xander didn't need to marry to preserve a family image…

In those first few raw days after he'd dumped her, she'd lived in a cold uncomprehending fog. She would wake hoping it had all been a bad dream and stretch her fingers out, hoping to find him there.

On the fourth day she'd checked her cell phone for the hundredth time, praying for word from him. At that exact same moment her mother had walked into her room. Elizabeth had looked from the cell in her hand to the woman who'd raised her, and the rose-coloured glasses she'd worn all her life had slipped off.

Romance and everlasting love were myths. Her parents were prime examples of this truth and she'd been a naïve idiot to think she would be any different.

From that moment her life changed. Everything.

Over the subsequent years she'd *refused* to think of the man who'd broken her heart. As far as she'd been concerned, he didn't exist, which worked for three years until she stumbled on a profile article about the newly appointed head of Timos SE, Xander

Trakas. Xander had managed the seemingly impossible and broken into the American market.

Reading it, she'd learned exactly how wealthy he and the Trakas family were, and how powerful; on a par with the Onassis family. It was through this article she'd learned about Ana Soukis. His childhood sweetheart. Xander and Ana had been going to marry but Ana had tragically died in a car accident before they could exchange their vows.

Xander had been twenty when Ana died. The same age he'd been when he'd married *her*, the lying, cheating dirtbag.

Either he'd married Elizabeth when he was engaged to another woman or he'd married her when he should have been grieving the love of his life.

She'd burnt the article and thanked her lucky stars the lying, cheating scumbag had dumped her before it had been too late to get an annulment. She didn't think she would have been able to handle a divorce.

As much as she'd hated herself for doing it, she'd kept an eye out for his name over the years. Xander had never remarried. And why should he? He had women falling off his arm; even more women than she had thought possible if one believed *Celebrity Spy!*

Of all the men in the eye of the scandal's storm, Xander was the least affected. He had no need to find a wife.

She shouldn't be thinking of him, she told herself crossly, slipping into her bathroom and putting the plug in the tub.

After a fourteen-hour flight she felt grubby and completely out of sorts.

If Piper hadn't said what she had, Elizabeth wouldn't even be thinking of him.

Determined to shove him from her mind, she thought of Piper instead and wished with all her heart she could warn her away from Dante. Elizabeth hadn't matched them together. Their marriage was being born from a one-night stand that had resulted in a pregnancy. Elizabeth's services had been required only to make the poor woman over and turn her into a shining, sparkly wife who would look good on Dante's arm.

If she'd been asked to match Dante with anyone, Piper would have been the last woman on the list. She was much too sweet and naïve for the world she was being thrust into.

Just as she, Elizabeth, had once been too sweet and naïve.

She stripped naked and stepped into the steaming, frothy water, then lay back and closed her eyes.

Her cell rang.

Every atom in her body froze. Including her brain.

Then her heart kick-started, hammering against her ribs as if demanding attention.

Breathing deeply and keeping her eyes squeezed shut, Elizabeth did something she had never done before and ignored it.

Eventually it rang off to voicemail.

A short vibration a moment later told her the caller had left a message.

She opened her eyes and gazed up at the white ceiling she had painted herself, and willed her body into calm.

It didn't have to be him. It could have been anyone. Her clients were the richest of the rich and not used to waiting for anyone. Most had no concept of personal space or personal time, not when it came to anyone but themselves. To them, she was employed to do a job and if they wanted to call her at ten p.m. on a Friday evening then she should damn well be available to take the call.

She would check the message when she got out and call whoever it was back. Her business was her baby and the one thing in her life she was proud of. She'd built it up from scratch and...

The cell rang out again.

This time her heart flew up her throat. She turned her head to stare at it. She'd placed it on the small ledge where she always put it, within arm's reach. The screen was flashing in time to the ring.

Before she could galvanise herself to do anything, it went through to voicemail again.

Within ten seconds it started ringing again.

A surge of adrenaline propelled her up. She wiped her hand on the towel on the sink then snatched the phone. It wasn't a number she recognised.

Her heart now gearing itself to fly out of her mouth, she put the cell to her ear.

'Hello?' she said tremulously.

'Elizabeth?'

Hearing Xander's deep voice in her ear was as

shocking as if she'd plunged herself into a bucket of ice. Her body reacted as if she had, the phone slipping from her rigid fingers and landing with a splash in the water between her legs.

Twenty minutes later, her blood pressure almost back to normal, her body dry and cocooned in a thick towelling robe, Elizabeth unplugged her hairdryer, which she'd blasted at the SIM card she'd yanked out of her sopping phone. Still cursing herself for her stupidity and hoping the damage was minimal, she inserted the SIM card into her old phone, which she'd dug out of a drawer.

It took three nail-biting minutes before she could confirm the switchover had been successful and that all her contacts had been saved. Unfortunately there was no way to track Xander's number on the old cell, but intuition told her it wouldn't be long before she heard from him again, and this time she would be prepared.

Her intuition was correct.

Her old cell still had everything set up on it, including emails. A message pinged into her inbox.

Elizabeth, it's Xander. I assume you're having issues with your phone. Here's my number. Call me as soon as possible.

Her first impulse was to burst into tears but, before they could be unleashed, anger so strong it burned flushed through her and dried the unshed tears in an instant.

So he *was* going to follow in the footsteps of his fellow Casanovas and employ her.

The *nerve* of him. The crassness. The complete lack of sensitivity.

What did *he* need a wife for?

As tempting as it was to fire an angry email back and tell him in graphic detail what he could do with his order to call him back *as soon as possible*, she held herself back.

Xander had left her ten years ago. If she were rude or ignored him it would imply that she was still angry with him, which in turn would imply she had never gotten over him, which in itself was ridiculous. She was simply tired and overwrought after a busy few weeks.

She would *prove* she didn't have any residual feelings for him.

She stood in front of her bedroom mirror and counted to thirty, then keyed in the number. It was answered on the first ring.

'Thanks for calling me back.'

His businesslike tone echoed into her ear.

Keeping her focus on her reflection, Elizabeth fixed a smile to her face so her complete lack of residual feelings for him echoed down the line. 'No problem. My apologies for earlier. I dropped my cell phone in Rome and it's been playing up since.' The lie fell smoothly from her tongue. Her voice sounded as friendly as she wanted it to be.

'Is it liable to cut out again?'

'No. I'm back home and have switched to my old one.'

'Good.' Without any pause he added, 'I need to see you.'

'Okay.' She dragged the word out to stop herself from screaming at him and then hurtling the cell down the toilet. Still smiling, she said, 'Do you have a particular date in mind?' If she could get out of this she would but her company—her very reputation—was built on her personal touch. She brought her own unique take to matchmaking and it was hugely successful. The staff she employed were for technical and clerical support only.

'I'm flying to your part of the world shortly. Are you available to meet tomorrow?'

Xander lived on a Greek island. Elizabeth made some swift calculations. It had to be almost six a.m. there. What time did the man get up?

Then she remembered the news stories. He probably hadn't gone to bed yet.

Or was he speaking to her *from* his bed? Did he have a woman asleep beside him at that very moment?

'Elizabeth?'

Swallowing back the sick feeling roiling in her stomach, she thought of her upcoming schedule. 'When you say tomorrow…?'

'Saturday. I should land around three p.m. Eastern time.'

'I have a lunch appointment tomorrow.'

'So you can do the afternoon.' It was a statement not a question and it set panic clawing through her.

'I'm free for the whole of Sunday,' she said, jumping at the chance to delay the meeting, even if only by a day. 'Do you know where my office is?'

'We won't be meeting there. I need you to fly out to meet me.'

Prickles made a slow crawl up her spine but she kept her tone breezy. 'Meet you where?'

'St Francis.'

All the air seemed to knock itself out of her lungs and the smile fell from her face.

'There won't be time to get my jet to New York to collect you, so I'll charter one to fly you over when your appointment's finished,' he continued. 'Pack an overnight bag and keep Sunday clear for me.'

She couldn't speak. Her brain had gone cold, her knees weakening enough that she shuffled back and sank onto the edge of her bed.

'Is there a problem, Elizabeth?' There was a hint of challenge in his businesslike tone.

She covered her mouth to hide the sound of herself clearing her throat, then said, 'There's no problem at all. I'll meet wherever it's most convenient for you.'

'St Francis is where it's convenient for me.'

'Are you aware I require a down payment of a quarter of my fee for overseas trips?' She strove to keep her voice composed and her breathing even.

'Message me your banking details and the amount, and I'll get it paid.'

Before she could think let alone voice any objection, he said, 'That's everything settled, then. I'll see you tomorrow.'

And then the line went dead.

She pulled the phone away from her ear and gazed at it as if it might suddenly bite.

Had that really just happened?

Billionaires throwing their weight around was nothing new. She was used to acting on their whims and fancies, had once conducted an interview with a client in a luxury Saharan Bedouin tent less than twelve hours after his initial call. To reach billionaire status required a ruthlessness mere mortals struggled to achieve. They weren't all bad people by any means but they were used to getting their own way and working to their own agenda, and she was used to complying with their whims. It was one of the reasons she'd become such a hit in their world.

Her conversation with Xander was a variety of one she'd held dozens of times with other clients. It hadn't been anything special. They were strangers who happened to have been married once and spent a grand total of fourteen days together. He clearly had no residual feelings for her, just as she had none for him.

It was the destination of St Francis that had thrown her into a funk.

Of all the places in the world, why there? *Why?*

It couldn't be coincidence that her ex-husband had chosen the very island where they'd met, married and separated to employ her services in finding him a new wife.

* * *

Xander disconnected the call and sighed heavily. He walked to his window and looked out over the Aegean, where the sun's first rays bounced on the horizon between the lightening sky and the still dark sea.

That was a call he'd hoped to not have to make. After the furious row with his parents that had gone on into the early hours, he'd come to the conclusion he had no other choice.

For his nephew's sake he needed a wife and he needed one now. It was sheer chance that he already had one.

All he had to do was convince Elizabeth to go along with it. After the way he'd ended things between them all those years ago, he knew he had a fight on his hands to get it. He could handle it. He was used to battles. Every day of his life was one.

He'd heard her sharp inhalation when he'd mentioned their destination. He'd deliberately kept their conversation short and to the point so she wouldn't have time to object. He would not give her the time or place to reject his proposal.

Elizabeth wasn't the girl he'd fallen for all those years ago who wore her heart on her sleeve and her emotions on her face. She'd matured into a discreet, professional woman with a cool analytical head.

She would need that cool head if she were to make the correct decision and agree to be his wife again.

CHAPTER TWO

THE PRIVATE JET Xander had chartered for her circled
St Francis's small airport. Elizabeth gripped the hand
rest. It wasn't fear of landing that made her knuckles whiten but fear of what the evening would bring.

She'd had one night to dream up something inven-
tive to get out of it; family emergency, car accident,
diabetic coma… She'd rejected every one of them.

When all was said and done, this was her job. Her
services were discreet and known only to a select
few, but those select few inhabited their own world.
All it would take was one whisper of unprofession-
alism or unreliability and the reputation she'd spent
eight years building up would be smashed down.

The Xander she'd known didn't exist. All she
knew of the real Xander was his reputation, and that
was of a man who didn't suffer fools. If he had any
affection left for her he wouldn't have insisted they
meet at St Francis.

She'd loved him once, with the whole of her heart.
The morning she'd packed her suitcase full of excitement at the thought of flying to Diadonus, the island

he lived on, to meet his family and begin their new life together, he'd pulled the rug out from under her. He'd told her that he'd made a mistake; that he didn't love her, his family would hate her and he'd be returning to Diadonus alone.

Her lungs and stomach contracted into balls as the pain of that moment hit her afresh. But she would give anything to live it again, so she could keep her composure and not have his last memory of her being one where she could hardly breathe through the tears.

In their short time together on this island she would show nothing but her professional face. She would be polite and friendly. She would treat him exactly as she would any other client. She would smile and pretend he wasn't a lying cheat who'd broken her heart.

The jet landed smoothly but that didn't stop the nausea increasing. She hadn't been this nervous since she'd walked out of her home and into the big wide world alone and unsupported.

The early evening sun still blazed over the pristine airport, casting the ground and small white terminal in a golden haze. She stepped off the jet, holding tightly to her carry-on case, purse and laptop bag. After the freezing New York temperatures, the warmth was welcome.

Before she'd travelled to St Francis, Elizabeth had never left the States, had hardly left New York. Then her granny had died and left some money for her only grandchild, her will stipulating clearly that she wanted Elizabeth to use some of it 'to get out of this darn country and see something of the world'.

Her granny would be delighted to know Elizabeth's work took her all over the world. And of all the places she'd been, this exclusive Caribbean island remained in her mind as the most beautiful place on earth…but the memory was tainted. It was as if the fine white sand had become tiny shards of glass and the clear blue Caribbean Sea, so enticing and welcoming, filled with poison.

An official in a golf buggy greeted her, gave her passport a cursory glance and whisked her off to the car park.

A rugged black four-by-four gleamed beside the terminal wall. At their approach, the driver got out, the setting sun enveloping him in the same haze as the surroundings.

Her heart leapt and her throat closed. It was Xander.

He strode towards her, his long legs covered by a pair of tan chinos, a short-sleeved pale blue shirt stretched across his honed torso, the brown hair she remembered as rumpled now cropped with a slight quiff at the front.

Her grip on her case tightened. He reached them, nodded at the driver and then fixed the sparkling blue eyes she'd once gazed into without blinking for what had seemed like hours on her…

Her insides turned to jelly. From deep in her chest a swell erupted; that awful need to burst into tears and sob. Where it came from she didn't know, but she controlled it. She'd known this wouldn't be easy and, she told herself, this would be the worst of it. That first time seeing and speaking to him again. That was always going to be the worst part and no amount of preparation could mitigate it.

'Elizabeth,' he said by way of greeting, stretching out a hand.

She'd always loved how he pronounced her name. Her mother always affected an English accent when she said it. Her father always addressed her as Lizzy but she suspected that had always been to needle her mother. From Xander's wide, generous mouth, her name rolled like a caress.

There was nothing wide or generous about his mouth now, fixed as it was in a tight line.

Plastering the brightest, most toothsome smile she could muster to her face, she released her hold on the case and accepted his hand. 'It's great to see you again.'

His lips curved into a taut smile. 'You're looking well.'

'Thank you.' Still holding his hand, she used it for support to climb out of the golf buggy, pretending that every inch of her skin hadn't started dancing at his touch.

He was as tall as she remembered but the years had given an added hardness to his physique and he'd gained an overall edginess she didn't remember from before. The sparkle that had always been in his eyes was muted and faint lines had appeared on his face, yet somehow he was even better looking than he'd been a decade ago.

So gorgeous had he been that when he'd approached her on her arrival at La Maison Blanc Hotel and insisted on helping her with her luggage, she'd assumed he worked for the hotel. In hindsight, that he'd been wearing a pair of swim shorts and had had a towel slung over his shoulder should have been a giveaway that he was a guest rather than a hotel porter. That, and the fact the other porters had been wearing navy blue uniforms, right down to the silly hats they were forced to wear. Xander's brown hair had been damp from a swim in the sea.

It had taken her a good ten minutes—enough time to check in and find her room—before she'd realised the drop-dead gorgeous young man with the infectious smile, sparkling blue eyes and a deep rich accent to die for wasn't an employee but a fellow guest, and that he was helping her because he was interested in her. In *her*!

They'd arranged to meet at the pool bar an hour later. By the time she'd unpacked and changed she'd convinced herself she'd dreamt him up. But there he had been, exactly where he'd promised. Two cocktails later and she'd learned he was Greek, twenty years old, and a single traveller like herself. Dreamer that she was, she'd been *convinced* fate had brought them together.

'Is this everything you've brought with you?' Xander asked, taking in the physical changes time had brought on his wife. He'd known she would have changed over the years but he hadn't expected it to be quite so profound.

Ten years ago she'd had the rounded features of a young woman. Now she was leaner, her cheekbones more defined. Large dark glasses stopped him seeing her eyes but she had a polish to her, a sophistication far removed from the wide-eyed ingénue who had captured his attention from the very first glance. That Elizabeth had been a fresh-faced open book.

This Elizabeth, the rampant curls he remembered straightened and glossed into long, tumbling waves, was professional and collected. She was dressed in slim-fitting dark grey jeans with studs across the pockets, and a fitted white shirt, which together emphasised her litheness. She could be anywhere, at a semiformal business meeting or out with friends for lunch. She was the perfect chameleon. Her looks were too striking for people not to look twice at her but she would fit in perfectly wherever she happened to be.

He carried her case to his Jeep. Elizabeth easily kept pace with him. He'd forgotten how long her legs were, and lengthened further by a pair of simple yet sexy black heels.

She was sexy. The way she carried herself. Her confidence. She was dazzling.

He pulled the passenger door open and waited until she'd taken her seat before closing it. Through the slight breeze he caught her delicate scent, which put the frangipani and butterfly jasmine St Francis was famed for to shame.

'I've booked us a table at a restaurant on LuLu Beach,' he said as he drove them out of the small airport, which mostly consisted of a landing strip and a pristine white hut. St Francis was one of the smaller Caribbean islands and had a colourful beauty that was world renowned. Not for nothing was it known as a honeymooner's paradise.

He'd chosen St Francis for a myriad reasons. It hadn't occurred to him that being on the island again would unsettle him so much. Sitting next to Elizabeth only unsettled him further, something he should have anticipated.

'Sounds good,' she said in the same easy tone she'd greeted him with. Yet, despite her friendliness, he detected a frost around her.

He could be imagining it, he supposed, but he doubted it. Meeting an ex wasn't normally a big deal but what he and Elizabeth had shared had been different from all his other relationships.

His honesty when he'd left her had verged on brutal but he'd known it was necessary. If he'd strung it out it would have hurt her a lot more.

Had she kept quiet about their annulment's failure as a means of punishing him; to make a bigamist of him if he'd married again? Had she spent a decade quietly biding her time for revenge?

Or did she genuinely not know they were still married?

He would learn the truth soon enough. Either way, a clean break had been the right thing to do and he had no regrets on that front. He'd disconnected the call from his mother and looked at the woman he'd married five days before and understood what a terrible mistake he'd made. His world was cut-throat and ruthless. If a woman raised in it like Ana couldn't cope, what chance would a dreamer like Elizabeth have? She would never have been accepted or fitted into it.

It wasn't long before they arrived at the LuLu Beach restaurant.

A waitress led them out to the terrace and to a table overlooking the beach. They sat opposite each other, both getting a good view of the tranquil surf lapping at the fine white sand like a loving puppy.

'Water for me,' Elizabeth said when asked what she wanted to drink.

'Water?' Xander queried.

'Water.'

He shrugged and turned to the waitress. 'One water and one bottle of beer.'

Once they were alone again he openly studied Elizabeth. The setting sun made the honey of her hair look like spun gold. 'You look as though life has treated you well.'

He wished she would take those damned sunglasses off so he could see her eyes and gauge what she was really thinking. The sun was now set so low its glare reflected directly off them.

'Thanks.' Elizabeth resisted the urge to say she knew life had been treating *him* well. After all, Xander's life had been all over the news and Internet for weeks.

She took a breath to calm the unexpected rage shooting through her.

Xander was her client and her clients' private lives were none of her concern. The salacious stories about the other three men hadn't bothered her in the slightest and she would not allow the burn that ravaged her brain whenever she imagined Xander acting out some of the described racier acts to cloud her judgement or control her emotions.

She'd thought she was prepared for this and for seeing him again but the racing of her heart and the dampness of her palms proved it to be a lie. She could have had a month to prepare and she still wouldn't have been ready.

The waitress returned with their drinks then pulled her notepad out to take their food order. Elizabeth ordered the Yellowfin Tuna Tartare appetiser. She wasn't hungry but it would be good to have something to nibble on, a distraction. Like most of the restaurants on the island, LuLu's menu was a mixture of French and Creole. She'd adored the fusion when she'd been here before. She'd actively avoided both since. She'd avoided anything that would bring the memories back.

'Why did you want to meet here?' she asked, glad the sun was still strong enough to warrant keeping her shades on. She'd read once the eyes were the gateway to one's true emotions. She couldn't bear to think of Xander looking into hers and seeing the pain all the bittersweet memories were evoking.

'It bothers you?'

'It bothers my pride. I have no issue finding a life partner for you but I do think you could have shown some sensitivity and chosen somewhere neutral for us to meet.'

'I don't require a life partner. I require a wife.'

'Is that not the same thing?'

'A life partner suggests permanency. I only need a temporary wife.'

Removing her professional notebook from her bag, Elizabeth wrote 'temporary marriage' in it and circled it so heavily the nib of her pen bent.

Determined as she was to keep things on a professional footing, she couldn't help but say, 'Using your ex-wife to find you a new wife is one thing, but conducting the preliminary interview on the very island we met and married screams insensitive jerk to me. You have the money and resources to travel anywhere your heart desires so why here? Was it to rub my nose in it?'

When she finally looked at him, he was staring at her with a look she couldn't interpret.

'I had a number of reasons.'

She forced herself to remain poised. If he wanted to play mind games he could play them on his own. She was here to do a job and nothing else. 'Tell me what kind of woman you have in mind to marry. Are there any turn-offs I need to avoid, like smokers or bearded ladies?'

Or five-foot-eight blondes with a pedigree your mother wouldn't approve of.

She wished she had a chain-smoker with the world's worst halitosis on her books to fix him up with.

Elizabeth waited for him to answer but his gaze remained on her, the same unfathomable expression on his gorgeous face.

Uncertainty crept up her spine. The way he was looking at her...

He took a swig of his beer then set the bottle steadily on the table.

'I don't need you to find me a wife, Elizabeth. I already have one.' He leaned forward and lowered his voice. 'There is no easy way for me to say this but you're still my wife. Our marriage was never annulled. We're still married.'

Xander watched the blood drain from Elizabeth's face.

Long moments passed before she gave a quick shake of her head and finally removed her shades.

The dazzling amber eyes Xander had never forgotten finally met his, flecks of gold and red firing at him, disbelief resonating. Not even a professional actress could fake shock that well. It put the last of his doubts to rest. She hadn't known.

Although the compression in his chest loosened a little at this, it made no difference to how things needed to proceed.

'Elizabeth?'

Her throat moved. Her words came out in a croak. 'Our marriage was annulled.'

'Our annulment was rejected by the judge at the last hurdle.'

Blinking rapidly, she put her sunglasses back on and pushed them up to sit atop her head. 'You're not joking, are you?'

He shook his head and watched her slump in her chair.

She inhaled heavily. 'I don't get it.'

Xander had a two-week heads up on it and he still didn't understand. 'Did you ever receive official confirmation?'

Her eyes were wide and bewildered before she put her elbows on the table and rubbed at her forehead. 'I received confirmation of the paperwork. I remember that. I remember it saying it would be rubber-stamped within a month, or whatever the time frame was.' She looked back at him. 'It was ten years ago. I don't remember all the details.'

'But you don't remember receiving the official annulment?'

'I...' She slumped some more. 'I moved out.'

'Moved out from where?'

'My mother's. I left home soon after I received the confirmation letter. Mom was supposed to forward all my mail to me but she didn't. I ended up having to redirect it myself.' She straightened and let out a forced shaky laugh, muttering, 'I can't believe her.'

Their marriage had been too short-lived to get to the 'meet the parent' stage. They'd both been so wrapped up in each other they'd hardly spoken of their families. All he'd known of hers was that her parents were divorced and she was an only child.

She'd taken a vacation to St Francis on the back of an inheritance she'd received from her paternal grandmother.

Elizabeth shook her head, trying to clear it of all the noise crowding in it. She felt as if she could explode. She shoved her chair back and got to her feet. 'I need to walk.'

He stayed seated, a set look on his handsome face, his blue eyes turning to steel as they held hers. 'You can walk later. Right now we need to talk.'

Her stomach clenched and there was a moment she feared she would bring up the morsel of food she'd managed to eat since their phone call the evening before.

Being with Xander again was a thousand times harder than she'd imagined and learning they were still married...

It wasn't possible. It wasn't.

Yet somehow it was.

Swallowing a ragged breath, she sat back down heavily.

The sun had almost set, its orange crescent gleaming over the horizon, the sky a deep blue shining with stars peeking out and waving at them. Such a beautiful sight and one that felt sacrilegious with all the turmoil Xander had just thrown her into.

Their food was brought to them. Xander had ordered monkfish fillets. The delicious scent from it turned her stomach.

Elizabeth looked at her tuna tartare, beautifully

presented with an avocado salad, and knew she wouldn't be able to manage even a bite of it.

'Why was the annulment denied?' she asked, trying frantically to get a grip on herself.

'The judge determined there were *"no unknown facts from either party"* and that *"no law had been broken"* so there was nothing to justify it.'

'But we were only married for five days.'

He sighed. 'Another judge would probably have rubber-stamped it without any issue. We were unlucky that ours landed on the desk of a judge who took issue with it. We'll never know his real reasons why—he passed away four years ago. How did you not *know* the annulment was declined?'

'I never received the letter.' Her mother had probably thrown it away unopened in a fit of pique.

'You've already said that, but why didn't you chase it? It seems strange that you didn't call or do something to find out where the confirmation was.'

'The same could be said for you,' she retorted, removing her gaze from the sunset to look at him. 'Didn't you think you would receive something too?'

'Hardly. I live on the other side of the world. You said you would handle it. As I recall, you insisted.'

'How long have you known?' she asked tightly.

'Just over two weeks.'

She clenched her fists to stop herself from lashing out at him. 'You've waited that long to tell me?'

'I was trying to work out the best way forward. I only looked into it because I was hoping to bury the annulment so the press wouldn't find out.'

'Why would you do that?'

'The press are digging into every aspect of my life. I knew it would only be a matter of time before they stumbled onto it. I thought it best to bury it completely before they found it and used it as additional ammunition to hit me with. My family don't know about us…'

'You never got round to telling them? What a surprise.' She didn't bother hiding her sarcasm. *My family will never approve of or accept you.*

She hadn't told her own family either but that had been for entirely different reasons. She hadn't been ashamed of Xander. She'd just been too humiliated and heartbroken to speak of it. She couldn't have endured hearing her mother's condemnation and her father's fake concern on top, then the fights as they tried to find ways to blame the other for it. Because it was always about them, never about her.

'Things are hard for us at the moment without having to deal with all the press intrusion,' he said.

'Am I supposed to feel sorry for you?' He'd been engaged to another woman. He'd used her and lied to her and then dumped her in the cruellest way possible.

'You're not supposed to feel anything. I'm just telling you how it is.'

'But you had to fly me all this way to tell me? You could have told me in New York—you could have told me *anywhere*. It seems particularly cruel to bring me to the island we were married on just to discuss our divorce. Well, you have nothing to worry about. I have more to lose than you if our marriage comes out and I want it buried just as much as you...'

'If I wanted a divorce I would have been in touch two weeks ago.'

Shaking off the fresh dread crawling up her spine at his words, Elizabeth said tightly, 'You went through the court records specifically to bury our marriage.'

'That was my original intention,' he agreed easily although his eyes remained hard. 'Learning we were still married changed things.'

The dread had lodged into her throat, suffocating her vocal cords so all she could do was plead with her eyes. *Don't say it. Whatever you do, don't say it.*

'I need us to rekindle our marriage.'

CHAPTER THREE

HIS MEANING HIT Elizabeth immediately, no initial instant of uncomprehending shock, no moment of bewilderment. 'Not in a million years.'

'You're a matchmaker, Elizabeth,' he said calmly. 'You arrange marriages…'

'For other people,' she interjected.

'I want to employ you to rekindle ours. It won't be for ever, a few months at the most.'

A passing waiter noticed they hadn't touched their food. 'Is everything all right? Can I get you anything?'

'I'd like a cab to the airport,' Elizabeth said.

Bemusement spread over the waiter's face. 'The airport's closed now.'

She'd completely forgotten flights were forbidden on or off the island after sundown.

'We'll have two coffees,' Xander cut in smoothly while she eyed him furiously.

'Cappuccino, latte…?'

'Two filter coffees will be fine.'

As the waiter drifted back inside, Elizabeth

leaned forward and glared at Xander. 'Is that why you brought me here? So I couldn't escape?'

'Partly. I had a number of reasons.'

'Well, guess what? I don't care what your reasons are. Keeping me here overnight isn't going to change my mind so you've lucked out there. I'm not doing it. Period.'

If he was perturbed by her vehemence, he didn't show it. Xander was treating the bombshell he'd just thrown at her as dispassionately as if he were conducting a business deal. She could be anyone to him, whereas for Elizabeth...

He had once been her world. Being with him again brought everything back. All of it. The delirious happiness followed by pain so sharp she had never allowed herself to get close to feeling either emotion again. They went hand in glove. If she hadn't known the joy she would never have suffered so much in the aftermath.

But it hadn't killed her. It had made her stronger and she would hold on to that strength.

'You don't even need a wife,' she said in a much calmer tone than the explosion her tongue wanted to fire. 'Your business has been completely unaffected by the *Celebrity Spy!* scandal...'

'It has nothing to do with my business.'

The waiter wandered back to them with their coffees, eyeing their still untouched plates with obvious confusion.

Once alone again, Xander stirred a spoonful of brown sugar into his cup and then fixed his eyes on her. 'My sister-in-law is an alcoholic. She's recently been diagnosed with cirrhosis of the liver. If she doesn't stop drinking she will be dead within five years.'

'You're talking about Katerina?' Elizabeth asked, shocked at this revelation.

His brow furrowed. 'You remember her name?'

Feeling her body heat under his narrow-eyed scrutiny, she took a hasty sip of her coffee.

How embarrassing to remember the name of a woman she'd never met who had probably been mentioned only the once, and in passing at that. But she remembered every conversation between them, had committed to memory the names of his family members. She'd looked forward to meeting them and being a part of their lives.

'Yes. I'm talking about Katerina,' Xander continued when Elizabeth didn't bother to answer his question. 'I don't know what will happen to her or if she will be able to stop drinking. I just don't know. But what happened to her has acted as a wake-up call to my brother. I have been begging him for years to get help for his addictions.' He gave a small tight smile. 'Yanis's poison of choice is cocaine, but he's not fussy. If it comes in white powder form he'll snort it. If it comes in liquid form he'll inject it.'

Now he reached for his coffee and cradled the cup in the same manner Elizabeth was cradling hers.

'Yanis admitted himself into a specialist lockdown facility in America ten days ago.'

The facility in Arizona was supposed to be one of the best in the world. Xander hoped with all his heart it could help his brother. If not…

He didn't want to witness his brother's coffin being lowered into the cold ground. He'd watched Ana's body be lowered and the grief and guilt had almost sliced him in two. He couldn't go through the same with his own flesh and blood, the only adult in his family he felt any affection for.

'That's good,' Elizabeth said in a softer tone. The stoniness of her eyes had softened a little too.

'It is. Very much so. He'll be in rehab for around two months. As Katerina is unlikely to leave hospital any time soon and will not be in a position to look after their son, Yanis left Loukas in my care.'

'Loukas is your nephew?'

Xander nodded. 'He's eight. Despite all the crap he's had to put up with, he's a great kid.' And now he'd come to the real reason he needed her. 'My parents have hired a lawyer to go for custody of him.'

Elizabeth's brows drew together. 'Custody of Loukas?'

'Yes. Full custody. They're saying Yanis and Katerina are unfit parents.'

He could see her brain whirling before she tentatively said, 'Is giving them custody really a bad thing? What, with the way your brother and Katerina are…?'

'It is the worst thing,' he stated flatly. 'My brother, when he's not high, is a good father. He's doing everything he can to straighten himself out so he can care properly for his son. My parents have made this move knowing full well that neither Yanis nor Katerina are in a position to fight it, so I must fight on their behalf.'

'But…'

'Elizabeth, I will not allow my parents to take custody of him. I wouldn't allow it even on a temporary basis.'

'Where's Loukas now?'

'At my home. I have a court order granting me temporary custody for two more weeks and then there will be another hearing. Now they know they're fighting me, my parents will go for the jugular. They will paint me as an unfit guardian too.'

'Why?'

'To stop me from winning. This scandal couldn't have come at a worse time. It's painting me as someone debauched and without any morals. The only way I'll be able to convince the court to let me keep guardianship of Loukas and fight Yanis's corner is if I can prove I have a stable home for him, and that's why I need us to rekindle our marriage. Having you as my wife will prove I'm a stable influence and kill my parents' plans.'

'It's that simple?'

'Sure.' He took a sip of his coffee. 'My country is still inherently conservative with a bias towards female carers. With you as my wife, they will see two people able to care for Loukas until his parents are well enough to take him back. If my parents get custody, they will never give him back.'

Her eyes clouded. 'Are they really likely to do that?'

'Without doubt. My family has been at war for years and my parents think they finally have a chance of winning a battle.'

Elizabeth removed her shades from the top of her head and folded the bows, her eyes distant, not looking at him, clearly weighing up everything he'd just shared.

'It really is quite simple,' he said. 'You and I announce our marriage to the world and stay together long enough for Yanis to get straight. With any luck, Katerina will make the road to recovery too.'

'And what if Yanis gets straight but then relapses?' she challenged. 'Will I be expected to act as your wife again?'

He shook his head. 'As soon as he's released from his facility, I'll get the steps put in place that I am to be Loukas's legal guardian in the absence of his parents. You and I will stay married until this has been done. Yanis will agree. If we'd known our parents would take this action we would have done it before but neither of us imagined even they would stoop so low. They hardly know Loukas.'

They *should* have imagined it, Xander thought grimly. His parents were a law unto themselves. They treated family life as they treated business: as a sport in which there could only be one winner.

'As I said, it's a simple matter of us rekindling our marriage. I appreciate it's asking a lot of you...'

'A lot?' she exclaimed, blinking furiously. 'My

business will be finished. Everything I've worked for…gone. It works on discretion, remember? And what about the rest of my life?'

'What life, Elizabeth? All you do is work.'

At the darkening of her features, he figured he might as well get everything out in the open and deal with it all in one go. 'I had you investigated. There's no significant other in your life. You have some friends you socialise with occasionally and you take yoga classes when time allows, but there is nothing else. So tell me, what will you be giving up to help me?'

Now her face was ablaze with outraged colour. 'You went digging into my life? Well, that explains how you discovered Leviathan Solutions.'

He was unrepentant. 'I learned about your business when searching for our annulment. I had a deeper search made to be sure you had nothing in your past that could be used to paint you as an unsuitable guardian for Loukas.'

As it was, his investigations hadn't revealed anything. If she had skeletons in her closet, they were tucked too far out of reach for discovery. If she'd dated anyone unsavoury, that was hidden away too. Indeed, he hadn't found evidence of a link with *anyone*, not even a fling, never mind anything approaching a committed relationship. Whatever relationships she'd had in the past decade, they'd been conducted discreetly and that was all that mattered.

'I don't care what excuses you make, that's a gross invasion of my privacy,' she raged. 'It's inexcusable.'

'If you were in my position you would have done the same.'

'If I were in your position I wouldn't need to—your private life is splattered on the front page of every red top for the whole world to see.'

'I can assure you the vast majority of it is highly exaggerated, the rest of it lies,' he said icily.

'Of course it is.' Her sarcasm was delivered with extra bitterness.

His temper rising, Xander finished his coffee and carefully set the cup on the table before pointing to the beach. 'Do you see the man with the camera round his neck?'

She followed his gaze.

'That man is a paparazzo, tipped off by my assistant that we're here.'

Her face contorted into such anger she looked ready to explode.

'He has your name. He knows about Leviathan Solutions and the service you provide. He knows we're married. What the story that accompanies his pictures tells is for you to decide.'

Elizabeth listened to Xander's words and knew her world was crumbling around her.

He'd set her up.

Whatever happened between them, pictures of one of the Casanovas from the *Celebrity Spy!* scandal pictured in a Caribbean paradise with a woman purported to be his wife would beam around the world. It would be headline news.

'I can't believe you would do this.' She was so

angry she could hardly breathe. 'You say your parents have stooped low…you are exactly like them.'

He was unrepentant. 'I regret I've had to take these steps but everything I'm doing is for my nephew. If you say no to my proposal I have nothing left to play. I have nothing left to lose. My reputation can't be damaged any more than it already has been. Say yes and you'll be financially set for life. Thirty million dollars for you, and I'll pay off your staff too.'

Elizabeth listened with the feeling of talons being dragged over her skin and her head swimming in cold sludge.

Her business was finished. Her life—everything she'd built for herself—was over.

Once the world learned she was married to this Casanova and her face graced the front pages of all the glossies and all the major Internet search engines, no one would be able to risk using her discreet services any more.

As if on cue, the photographer put the camera to his eye and fired off a ream of shots of them.

She took a long breath and rose from the table, pulling herself to her full height. 'I would have agreed to do it without the threats and blackmail.'

'I couldn't take the risk you would say no. I haven't seen you in ten years. For all I knew you were holding a grudge against me. I had to consider if you'd deliberately withheld the failure of our annulment as a weapon to use against me when a time came that suited you.'

'*What?* How could you *think* such a thing?' She shook her head, trying to comprehend it. Ten years ago she'd laid herself bare to him, in all senses, and he thought her capable of something like *that*?

'Manipulation is a common thing in my world. I can count the number of people I trust on two fingers.'

'Well, you've certainly mastered the art of manipulation yourself,' she said bitterly. Where was the man she'd married? That man had been *nothing* like this.

A pulse throbbed in his jaw. 'I am trying to protect my nephew.'

'When adults go to war it's always the child who suffers the most.' She knew that better than anyone. 'I would never stand by and let it happen if there was something I could do about it. You didn't need to go to such grotesque lengths for my help. You didn't need to make me hate you more than I already do.'

'I'm sure the thirty million I'm offering will sweeten the pill.'

'No amount of money will recompense for the loss of my business and the invasion of my privacy.'

'You want more money?'

She caught the sneer on his lips, which only fuelled her fury further. 'Don't try and make me out to be a money-grabber,' she snapped. 'If you hadn't given *Celebrity Spy!* so much gossip to shout about, you wouldn't be in this mess and you wouldn't need me to get you out of it—your moral fibre wouldn't even be a matter of discussion. Your parents wouldn't be able to paint you as an unfit guardian.'

Another flash of anger resonated from his eyes but his lips formed into a taut smile. 'Your opinion of my character means nothing to me. All I want is your agreement. Do I have it?'

'I don't have any damn choice.'

'I'm pleased you can see that.'

'But let's get one thing straight. Our marriage will be as short as possible and strictly platonic.'

The pulse in his jawline throbbed harder. 'Married couples in my family share adjoining rooms. It's an arrangement that will suit us.'

'Good. And any adjoining door will have a lock.'

'Yes.' His eyes glinted through the darkness, impossible to read. He got to his feet and pulled some notes from his wallet. 'It's time to go—we have a hotel to check into.'

'*We?*'

'Yes, *kardia mou*,' he said with a mocking smile. 'We are setting the seeds for the rekindling of our marriage. We have been pictured dining together. That photographer has been given the name of our hotel. I guarantee you he has a scooter in easy reach for him to rush there and meet us. Come the morning, the world will know we have spent the night together. All that will be left for us to do is make a statement, which I have already prepared.'

'My God, you've planned *everything*.'

'You don't get to my position without forward thinking.'

'Really? I could have sworn you'd got to your position through a fate of birth.'

It gave fleeting satisfaction to see his face darken at that comment.

'But really, Xander, is this necessary? Do you really think your parents are going to be fooled by us getting back together when they didn't even know I existed? Don't you think they'll find it convenient?'

When he replied his voice was tightly controlled. 'It's not my parents we need to convince, it's the judge, and, unless you want to forfeit the money, I suggest you make it *very* convincing.'

'You have got to be kidding me.' Elizabeth's voice was flat but her amber eyes blasted incredulity and fury right at him.

Xander brought the car to a stop at the front of La Maison Blanc Hotel. 'Is there a problem?'

'Why here?'

'Because it's fitting. This is where we married and now it's where we're rekindling our marriage.'

'And to hell with my feelings, eh?' She shook her head with loathing. 'Just when I didn't think it was possible to hate you more…'

'Hate me as much as you want in private, but in public…' He nodded at the scooter that had come to a screech at the hotel's entrance.

She sucked in her cheeks and contemplated the photographer, whose camera was still around his neck. 'This is pointless. No one's going to believe we're for real, especially not a judge. I *hate* you.

And you never even mentioned me to your family or...'

'I never mentioned you to anyone because the topic was too painful,' he cut in smoothly. 'We never wanted to part but we were too young at the time and we knew it would never work. You called me when the scandal first erupted to offer your support. My world was falling apart around me and you were there for me.'

He stretched out a hand to touch her face. The soft, almost translucent skin still felt like satin to his touch. Before she could flinch away he wound his fingers round the back of her head and gathered a large mass of her thick hair into his fist. He wondered what had happened to her curls. He'd adored the shaggy mop of hair she'd sported a decade ago.

'It was in the course of one of our discussions that we realised our annulment had never gone through and we were still married.' He leaned closer and studied the soft kissable lips that were pressed tightly together sucking in the rounded cheekbones.

Did those lips still taste the same? Would they still fit to his as if they'd been moulded specially?

She'd stopped breathing. Her eyes had widened, her face a frozen mask.

Still gazing at her mouth, resisting the urge to run a finger over it, he continued, 'It was also through the course of our talks on the phone that I remembered how special you were to me and all my old feelings for you came back. I convinced you to meet me here because I wanted to see if the old magic was still alive. We realised how much we still loved each other and decided that we'd both matured enough to make our marriage work.'

He released his hold on her hair and let his fingers drift down the slender neck he had once kissed every part of, and felt the tiniest of shivers under his fingers.

Her eyes were wide and stark on his.

A long-forgotten memory sluiced him; their first time together, her dreamy pleasure, her soft moans…

The flash of the photographer's camera cut through the moment and pulled him back to the present.

He removed his hand from her neck.

Elizabeth might have an allure that sang to his senses but this was one relationship he had no intention of taking to the bedroom. Things were going to be difficult enough between them without throwing sex into the mix.

It gave him no pleasure to threaten and blackmail her but he couldn't afford to give her a way out. Loukas was all he cared about and he would do whatever it took to keep his nephew out of his parents' clutches, even if it meant destroying the woman he had once thought himself in love with.

CHAPTER FOUR

'OH, THAT IS very clever,' Elizabeth whispered after a long pause during which her breathing deepened. 'Machiavelli would be proud.'

Xander didn't say a word. What *could* he say?

It wasn't for ever, he told himself in mitigation. A few months of her life at the most, and he would pay her handsomely for it.

'Just tell me how you plan to explain Ana.'

His stomach lurched. 'You know about her?'

Throughout the years, whenever an unguarded moment found him thinking of Elizabeth, he would wonder if she'd learned of Ana. He'd never spoken of Ana to the press but occasionally an article would appear that mentioned his tragic fiancée.

When Xander had ended his engagement, he hadn't hung around to deal with the fallout. He'd been sick of everything: his family, her family... He'd needed a break from it all. And so he'd found himself in St Francis, where he'd met Elizabeth.

She'd been a ray of light that had beamed straight into his heart, a loving innocent when he'd only known indifference and manipulation. In the greedy haze of lust he'd been certain he was in love with her. He'd been unaware that his and Ana's families had postponed the statement about the end of the engagement, both families *convinced* he was suffering from nothing more than cold feet and would realise the error of his ways on his return and marry Ana after all.

Ana had known he would never change his mind.

The call from his mother notifying him of Ana's death had brought him crashing down to earth and he'd seen the truth right there in front of him: Elizabeth wouldn't have lasted a week with his family. All the joy and sunshine she brought into a room would have been snuffed out with the poison his parents and those they mixed with breathed.

'I know you were engaged to her,' Elizabeth said in a whisper. 'You were childhood sweethearts. And I know you never mentioned her to me. You told me…' She swallowed. 'You said you'd never been in love before. That was a lie.' Then she shook her head, her voice regaining a brisk tone. 'So how are you going to explain marrying me when you were engaged to someone else? How is that going to paint you in a respectable fashion?'

He didn't blink. 'I'd ended my engagement to Ana before I met you. She died while I was here with you. I didn't cheat on anyone. When I met you I was single. I couldn't have predicted what would happen to her.'

Xander knew he sounded cold. Thinking of Ana

and what happened to her always made him *feel* cold. He would never know what had been going through her head the night she died but knew he would carry the guilt for ever.

For a long time Elizabeth did nothing but stare at him. And as he stared back, a pain settled in his chest as he recalled her devastation when he'd walked away.

'Is that the truth or another clever statement you've concocted?' she asked coldly.

'It's the truth. Ana and I were over when I met you.'

She inhaled deeply, then gave a sharp nod and, without uttering another word, opened her door. She took hold of her belongings, and got out of the car, handing her stuff to the porter who had rushed to meet them.

Alone in the car, Xander closed his eyes.

Elizabeth really *had* changed.

Ten years ago she'd been easy to read. Everything she thought or felt was there in those amber eyes. He couldn't read them now. She'd built a wall around herself, a guard he suspected she rarely let anyone see beneath.

This wall would stand her in good stead. But it wasn't just the wall she'd built; she'd developed a tough core.

The old sweet Elizabeth would have been destroyed to have his mother's venom turned on her. This Elizabeth wouldn't take crap from anyone. She would survive their short rekindling intact.

Filled with resolve that he was doing the right thing, he got out and threw the keys at the valet. With a camera flashing frantically in his face, he strode into the grand foyer.

It was time to play their romance to a wider audience.

Elizabeth was waiting at the reception desk. Reaching her side, he slipped an arm around her waist and gave his name to the receptionist, who wasn't quick enough to hide the widening of her eyes.

Even the inhabitants of tiny St Francis had heard of his so-called debauchery.

He signed the forms, and the key cards were handed over to them.

Elizabeth looked at hers, read the name of the villa they were staying in, and nearly dropped it.

'Enjoy your stay,' the receptionist said with a coo.

All she could give was a rigid smile in return.

Xander took her hand and tugged at it to get her moving.

Just about ready to kill him but determined to affect nonchalance with an audience watching, she let him lead her to the far door that would take her to the same private villa he'd upgraded them to after they'd married. The honeymoon suite.

They followed the same narrow rocky path they'd taken a decade ago, passed the same open-air restaurant with the same jazz music playing, the same sweet-smelling flowers as the path took them further from the main hotel, the same herbaceous borders, the same distant noise of crickets calling to each other…everything the same. Even her husband.

But Xander was no longer the irrepressible young hunk she'd fallen in love with. He was a hard-nosed, wildly successful businessman with a ruthlessness that made her mother look like an amateur.

And he'd never been in love with her. The most she'd been to him was a rebound fling that went too far.

The sights, scents and sounds opened up so many memories her head flooded with them. This first step to their villa was the place Xander had scooped her into his arms and carried her to their door. This villa door where he now swiped the key card was where he had put her down, pressed her against this very wall and kissed her so hard her lips had bruised. This threshold she now crossed was the same one he'd picked her back up to carry her over.

And this villa was the very same one they'd made love in so many times it had been impossible to keep count, right until he'd received one phone call and dropped her quicker than an outfielder letting an easy catch slip through his fingers.

She hadn't known it then but that call had been the one telling him his fiancée had died.

Was he telling the truth that he'd ended the engagement before he'd met her? Or was it just another strategy to accompany their charade?

What did it matter anyway? It had all happened a decade ago. It meant nothing to her now. She only felt so raw and unhinged because…well, because her life had just been devastated all over again by the same man who'd almost broken her before.

Holding her breath, she walked into the villa. Her stuff had been placed on the floor of the spacious living area next to a suitcase she assumed was Xander's, although she hadn't seen any sight of it until then.

'Where are the staff?' she asked stiffly. The villa came with its own butler, maid and chef.

'I've told them we want privacy. They won't come unless we call them.'

He'd done the same when they'd married, ensuring the utmost privacy for them. Back then she had rejoiced in it.

The villa had a large kitchen in the corner of the main living area.

Xander peered into the huge American fridge and pulled out a bottle of white wine. 'Drink?'

'No.' She nearly followed it with a thank you but stopped herself in time. She didn't owe him anything, least of all good manners. 'I'm going to bed. You're welcome to the master bedroom.'

She would rather swim with piranhas than sleep in that room. The second bedroom was every bit as nice and came with the added bonus of not being seeped in memories of them being together.

'We've only just got here.'

'The sooner I get to sleep, the sooner I'll wake up and can go back to New York.' She didn't want to think any more. Her head hurt too much to handle anything else. All she wanted now was a few hours of oblivion.

'We'll be flying directly to Athens.'

'You can. I need to go home. I have work.'

'Elizabeth, your home is with me now.' As he spoke he put the wine back in the fridge and took out a bottle of beer as replacement.

'I can't come with you yet. I have things to do, arrangements to make…'

'You'll have to do it remotely.' He opened a drawer.

'That's impossible.'

He rooted through another drawer and pulled out a bottle opener. 'I need to get back to Loukas. I promised him I wouldn't be longer than two days.' He fixed her with a stare. 'Or do you think I should break a promise to an eight-year-old boy?'

'That's not fair,' she protested. 'I didn't know you'd promised him that. Of course you must keep it, but your promise doesn't involve me. You go ahead and I'll fly over when my affairs are straight.'

'You will fly with me in the morning. The re-kindling of our marriage starts immediately. The longer we're together before the court hearing, the more established and stronger we will look as a couple.'

'My staff deserve better than to be laid off by email.'

'The money I'll transfer into their bank accounts will make up for it. Give me their details and I'll do it now. I'll also transfer a quarter of a million dollars into your account—call it a retainer. You'll get the balance when we go our separate ways.'

'And if we fail?' Was there a chance she could walk out of this nightmare and *still* lose everything?

His eyes narrowed.

'What happens to me if the judge gives your parents custody?' she persisted.

Xander's voice was like ice as he said, 'It will only come to that over my cold dead body.'

Elizabeth sat in the lotus position on the floor of her locked bedroom, eyes closed, willing her mind to clear and for tranquillity to seep into her consciousness.

It wasn't happening.

How could she find any peace of mind with Xander situated on the other side of the wall?

God, that was all that separated them. After ten years apart they now had nothing but a wall of bricks dividing them.

An hour after she'd left him swigging moodily from his beer bottle, she'd heard the faint sound of a shower running from the next room.

She hadn't heard anything from him since. That didn't stop her ears straining for any movement.

It was a struggle to take in everything that had happened over the past few hours. How could she not have realised the annulment was never finalised and they were still married? It defied credulity. But back then she'd had so many other things to deal with and she had never dreamt their annulment would be denied. How could any judge fail to give an annulment with the facts before them?

Turned out a judge could, and if she'd only taken the effort to make one phone call she wouldn't be in the mess she was in now.

Her life as she knew it was over, at least for the foreseeable future.

This time tomorrow, her business would be over permanently.

She'd dealt with major upheaval before. She'd left the path she'd originally chosen and taken a completely different route and not only survived but thrived. She could thrive again. When all this was over she would pick herself up and start again, just as she had before.

All she had to do to get out of this mess without being left flat broke was convince a Greek judge that she and Xander were a stable couple in love.

It would be easier to feign love with a rattlesnake and, she suspected, safer.

Her thighs aching and her brain still refusing to switch off, Elizabeth gave up her attempts at meditation and took a shower.

Just as wired after her shower as she'd been before, she accepted she could kiss any sleep goodbye. The walls of the room seemed to be compressing in on her, squeezing the air from her lungs. She needed to get out. She wished she could take a long walk.

Throwing on the robe provided by the hotel, she went to the door and turned the handle. She strained her ears but the only sound to be heard was her own heart pumping.

She took a deep breath and stepped out onto the

ceramic tiles, cautiously checking Xander's door. It was shut.

Ghostly moonlight poured in through the high windows and patio doors where the shutters hadn't been closed.

After a moment's indecision she crossed to the patio doors and stared out.

Cut into the mountains, the villa had the perfect view of St Francis Bay, which rippled gently in the near distance, matchstick figures walking hand in hand along the shore. She swallowed back the ache that formed to remember her and Xander doing that same moonlit walk.

Sliding the patio door open, she stepped outside and was immediately enveloped in the rich, balmy Caribbean night. The moon loomed huge in the sky, bathing everything in light.

The heady sweet scent of butterfly jasmine, always at its strongest in the midnight hours, filled the air. As she breathed it in, a lancing pain shot through her, so strong she flattened a hand against her stomach to counteract it. It was the scent that had sat the strongest in her memories of her time at St Francis and a scent she had actively avoided since because it always carried her back to the time before he'd rejected her, when she'd thought she'd found her soulmate.

Elizabeth had never felt as if she belonged to anyone as anything other than a possession to be fought over, but for two glorious weeks with Xander she had felt as precious and invaluable as any jewel.

And then he'd dumped her as if she were worthless and broken her heart as easily as if it had been made from glass.

Hearing movement behind her, she sighed and swallowed back a lump in her throat.

'Beautiful night, isn't it?' he said quietly, coming to stand beside her at the balustrade. He sounded different from earlier. Less edgy.

'It was.'

He laughed, a low rumbly sound that carried through the still air. It was the first sign of the old humour she had adored. 'Don't hate me, Elizabeth.'

She turned her head a fraction to look at him and immediately wished she hadn't. Xander was wearing nothing but a pair of low-slung black shorts. She could smell the citrusy scent of his shower gel. She could smell *him*, and closed her eyes tightly along with her breath.

In their time apart it wasn't just his shoulders that had filled out, it was all of him. The fit, lithe young man who could have been mistaken for a surfer dude was now a toned, muscular thirty-year-old. The years had hardened him but they'd also added a whole new testosterone-filled dimension.

An ache formed low in her belly, a liquid tightness that turned into a throb...

She turned her attention back to the beach. 'You could have just told me about Loukas from the start. It didn't have to be like this.'

'To guarantee your agreement, it did. I wasn't prepared to hear you say no and I didn't have the time to sweet-talk you into it.'

'I don't want your sweet talk.'

'I've figured that out for myself,' he said drily.

'Then you're smart enough to figure out that it's impossible for me not to hate you.'

'That is regrettable.' He rested his hands on the balustrade next to hers.

She looked down at them, so close to her own, and experienced another pang. His muscular arms were tanned and covered in sun-bleached fine hair that stopped at the wrists. The long, strong hands... how could she have remembered them in such detail, right down to the silvery scar on the left one? Was there not a single thing she'd forgotten even though she'd spent the last decade determinedly not thinking of him except in the most unguarded of moments?

At least her private thoughts weren't something his spies could have discovered.

Her body heated with the rise of humiliation at what they would have learned and relayed to Xander. While he was busy enjoying life to the full, bedding as many beautiful women as he could get his greedy hands on, she'd spent the intervening years alone. Not even a brief fling or two to even things out between them and stop her feeling like an English spinster in an old-fashioned novel.

God, she'd never even thought this way before. She'd been *happy* in her solitary life. She'd had her business. She'd employed some great people who were fun to be around and had some great friends.

She had enough money not to worry about starving and was able to splash out on the odd pair of her favourite designer's shoes whenever the mood took her.

But prying eyes wouldn't see this. All prying eyes would see was her retiring to bed alone every night.

She took a step back and jutted her chin. 'The only regrettable thing is that I ever met you in the first place.'

Without wishing him a good night—for she absolutely did not wish him anything other than a sleep full of bad dreams—Elizabeth went back into the villa and locked her bedroom door behind her.

CHAPTER FIVE

THE NEXT DAY Xander sipped at his strong coffee, watching Elizabeth work. As soon as his plane had taken off, she'd taken herself to the furthest point away from him, to the large oak desk in his study area. There she had spent the past three hours making calls and working on her laptop.

She'd dressed in a short black skirt topped with an oversized monochrome top, her long hair sleek and glossy and falling over her shoulders. Last night, when he'd found her on the balcony, her hair had been wet. When she'd stormed away from him he'd noticed little curls springing up where it was starting to dry.

He remembered her curls so clearly and his heart throbbed to know they were still there even if they were straightened to within an inch of their life. She must have risen before the sun to get ready.

As polished as she appeared, carefully applied make-up could not disguise the dark rings under her eyes.

Done with her call, she put her cell phone on the desk.

He rose and walked over to her. 'You should take a break.'

She didn't look at him, turning her attention back to the screen in front of her and tapping out a few words on the keyboard. 'When I'm finished.'

'Lunch will be served soon.' She hadn't eaten anything since she'd landed in St Francis, her tuna tartare from the night before left untouched.

'I'll eat while I work.'

Her cell phone rang out. She snatched it up and put it to her ear.

'Hey,' she said in a much softer tone than she used with him.

Seating himself on the rounded sofa, nonchalantly hooking an ankle on his thigh, Xander listened to her one-sided conversation.

'I'll get it finished within the next hour,' she was saying. Then she smiled. 'Really? That's great. I'd be lost without you.' More silence, then, 'I'll call you later, when I'm settled.'

'Who was that?' he asked when she'd ended the call.

'My PA.'

'How's she taking things?' He thought of the large wedge of money he'd transferred into her four members of staff's bank accounts.

'*He's* taking things fine.'

'You have a male assistant?'

'Yes. I call him my PA but, really, he's my right-hand man. Not only is he an excellent organiser but he's a whizz with technical stuff and can fix any of the gremlins our computer systems get with his eyes closed. Not that any of that matters any more.' She sighed.

'You work closely with him?'

'More than anyone else, yes. Steve's been with me pretty much from the beginning. He keeps the office running smoothly, which is just what I need as I travel so much. I couldn't have done it without him.'

'And is your relationship strictly professional?' Her tone with 'Steve' had been tender. Now he knew it was a male she'd directed that tone at he felt an inexplicable urge to crush something.

Her face darkened. 'Not that it's any of your business but that's a totally crass thing to ask.'

'It is my business and it's a natural thing to wonder about. You sounded very cosy speaking to him.' Had their relationship been so obvious, so right there in front of them that his investigators had missed it?

'Do not put me on the same level as you—not everything's about sex. Steve's my friend. I care about him. I care about all my employees. They're all waking up to find they've lost their jobs but, rather than taking the money and running, they're doing their best to help me wind the company up seeing as I'm going to be stuck in Greece for the foreseeable future and unable to do it myself, *and* they're fielding calls from panicking clients who are all suddenly terrified their relationships are about to be exposed. So don't even think of questioning my relationship with any of them. They're the best bunch of people I know.'

As Xander had promised, pictures of the pair of

them together had flooded the Internet, every gossip blog headlining with them. The photographer had got a good one of them in the car outside the hotel, when Xander's hand had been buried in her hair. They were gazing into each other's eyes.

Elizabeth had to admit, this picture would go a long way into making people believe they were in love. There was an intensity to their gazes that made her stomach do a funny turn.

It looked as if they were about to kiss.

She'd studied that picture for far too long, holding her breath as warmth spread through her veins until she'd clicked away from it with the tap of a shaking finger.

Two members of the cabin staff bustled through carrying trays of food.

'I'll eat here, thanks.' Elizabeth pushed her laptop to one side to make room for hers. Xander indicated for his to be placed there too and sat himself on the leather seat opposite her.

She didn't say anything, diving a fork into her salad and turning her attention back to her screen, determined to tune him out. It proved impossible.

Not wanting him to think he was affecting her appetite, she forced herself to eat. She was quite sure her Niçoise salad was the best salad she'd ever eaten but she couldn't taste any of it.

Another message hit her inbox. She read it with a sigh.

'A problem?'

She looked at the man responsible for this entire

mess. 'Nearly all my clients have terminated their contracts with me.'

Thanks to Xander tipping the paparazzo off, the whole world now knew about Leviathan Solutions. A member of his staff had released a statement that was practically word for word as he'd recited it in the car.

'You knew that would happen,' he reminded her.

'Yes, but I wanted to tell my current clients personally. They deserve that much.'

At least the other Casanovas from the *Celebrity Spy!* scandal were matched already. She was confident Benjamin and Julianna would work out. They might have been playing cat and mouse with each other but, along with all the other things that made them perfectly suited to each other, there was real chemistry between them.

As for Zayn...the ladies she'd matched him with had turned out to be surplus to requirements as the beautiful Amalia, a PA, had unexpectedly been given the role. From the whispers Elizabeth had heard, blackmail was involved in this marriage. Whatever the truth, having seen Zayn and Amalia together she'd decided that, unlike Dante and Piper, they were a couple she *would* have matched.

She closed her eyes and fought back bitter tears.

She'd known yesterday that agreeing to rekindle their marriage would mean the end of her business. She hadn't realised how swift its destruction would be.

'Have you transferred the quarter-million you promised me?' She didn't have her pass key to access her bank via the Internet; Steve had promised to get it couriered to her in Diadonus.

She hated how Xander's eyes narrowed at her question.

'My current clients have paid for a service I can no longer provide,' she explained hotly. 'I have to refund them. There's not enough in my account to pay it without that money.'

'It's been transferred.'

She sighed her relief and almost said thank you.

'What will you do with the rest of the money I give you?' he asked.

'I'll be earning that money. It won't be a gift.' By the time this was done, she would have earned every cent.

He quelled her with a stare. 'Thirty million dollars is more than you've earned in your career. I'd say it's a handsome pay-off for a few months' work.'

'Money isn't everything.'

'Tell that to the person who has nothing.'

Which was what *she* would have if they didn't pull this off.

'And if money means nothing to you, you would have turned it down.'

'Just because I'm not that materialistic doesn't mean I'm a fool. Once this is over I'll still have to eat. I'll still have a mortgage to pay.' She just wouldn't have her business. Her baby.

They'd talked of having babies, she remembered. They'd even chosen names. Imogen and Rebecca for the girls, Samuel and Giannis for the boys.

Leviathan Solutions was the closest thing to a baby she would have.

'You'll be able to pay your mortgage off.'

She shrugged. She wouldn't allow herself to think of what she'd do with the money until this was over and the money was sitting pretty in her bank account.

'How did you get into matchmaking?' he asked. 'You were going to be a writer.'

She forked a tomato and strove not to react. She hadn't imagined he would remember anything important about her.

What harm could it do to tell him? It didn't matter any more. The mystique she'd created around Leviathan no longer applied.

'Chance. I had a college friend from my Brown days whose family would only agree to him joining the family firm if he married. Mike loathed the idea but not enough to forego his place in the firm. Phoebe was a friend from my junior high days, working as a legal secretary and hating everything about her life—she came from old money but her family had frittered most of it away. All she wanted was to marry someone with enough money for her to quit work, and raise kids and sit on charity boards. Shallow, I know, but she's a really fun person to be around. Anyway, instinct told me they would be perfect for each other, and they were.'

'How did that translate into providing a matchmaking service for the elite?'

'Mike's part of the Garcia family.'

Comprehension dawned in his eyes. Garcia's was

one of the largest privately owned investment banks in the US. 'I see. And you went to college with Michael Garcia?'

'Yes. I stayed in touch with a lot of my friends from Brown when I transferred to New York State.'

'Why did you transfer?' When Xander had received his investigator's report on Elizabeth he'd been stunned to discover she'd transferred from the prestigious Ivy League Brown University to New York State. From the timings, it had happened soon after their time together on St Francis, right before she'd started her second year.

'Lots of reasons, none of which I want to discuss with you.'

Shutters had come down on her amber eyes.

Whenever he'd unwittingly thought of her over the years he'd imagined her sitting at a desk, surrounded by novels and notebooks, scribbling away. Yet, instead of majoring in English Literature as she'd planned and becoming a scriptwriter, she'd majored in business and set up a matchmaking company.

'Do you ever match people for love?' She'd been an incurable romantic when he'd known her, a believer in destiny and the alignment of stars.

Her honey hair swung around her shoulders as she shook her head. 'That's not what my company's about. What it *was* about. I brought together people who had specific needs in a partner which had nothing to do with love.' Her eyes met his. 'Both parties knew exactly what they were getting into. No lies.

No deceit. No unrealistic expectations. No broken hearts.'

Her words were loaded with meaning, all of it singing loud and clear.

'Doesn't love come into it?' he asked, refusing to believe the dreamer he'd met so long ago was completely gone.

She shook her head even more vigorously. 'If people are stupid enough to want to be matched for love then they can go elsewhere for help in finding it. It doesn't exist and I want no part in the destruction of their dreams.'

He contemplated her a little longer. Their thoughts on marriage aligned. Romantic happy ever afters were a nonsense. Hearing it from her lips though... it proved like nothing else that Elizabeth really had changed.

She was as cynical as he was.

Fourteen hours after leaving St Francis, they landed in Athens.

After years of travelling the world's time zones, Elizabeth still struggled to adjust to the major differences. Her exhausted body thought it was midnight and time to sleep. The early Greek sunshine begged to differ.

Adjusting her watch to seven a.m., she followed Xander through the airport where they were whisked through the official bits, and out into a car. A short drive took them to a smaller airport, where they climbed the steps into a much smaller plane for the short flight to Diadonus.

Small but perfectly formed, Diadonus was part of the densely packed Cyclades and unmistakably Greek. The clear blue skies brought a chill to the morning but the rising sun promised warmer weather ahead.

Another car met them on the landing strip and soon they were on their way to Xander's home.

'Will your parents be there?' she asked, voicing the fear in her belly that had been gnawing at her since they'd landed in Athens.

'No. They rarely come to Diadonus. It's unlikely you'll meet them before the court hearing.'

'Won't they come and visit Loukas?'

The smile he gave her was bitter. 'I can count on one hand the number of times they've visited him. Neither of them like it here. It's too quiet for their tastes.'

'But I thought you'd always lived here?'

'The Trakas family has always had a home here but my parents prefer Athens. When I took over the running of Timos they moved there full-time.'

'Do you live in the family home?'

'Yanis and Katerina have it. I had a new home built for me five years ago.'

The new home turned out to be a palatial white Mykonian-style villa set above a horseshoe-shaped beach. Elizabeth had visited many palatial homes during the course of her career, none of which failed to evoke her admiration. This was the first that properly took her breath away. It had such simplicity and cleanliness yet such beauty, and the *views*... Breathtaking.

The Aegean rippled close by, its white surf skimming the sandy beach, clusters of white homes nestled close to the shoreline in all directions but far enough away to ensure absolute privacy. Squinting when she got out of the car, she could make out another island in the far distance.

Her throat closing, she followed Xander up white concrete steps to the front entrance. Her few possessions were taken in by a member of his household staff who materialised from nowhere with a friendly smile.

They had barely stepped inside before a squeal sounded out and a small, skinny figure in rumpled navy pyjamas hurtled into the reception room to throw his arms around Xander.

Loukas.

Xander lifted him high into the air and planted kisses all over his nephew's face, to further squeals of delight.

It was only when he'd been placed back on his feet that Loukas noticed Elizabeth, hanging back a little, feeling decidedly like an intruder.

The happiness resonating from the blue eyes so like his uncle's turned to wariness and he visibly shrank into himself.

Xander noticed the change and crouched down. 'Loukas, this lady is my friend Elizabeth,' he said slowly in English. Like generations of Trakas children, Loukas had an English nanny to ensure he grew up bilingual, but in recent months his learning had taken a backwards turn. His teachers at the local school he attended—a break from the Trakas tradition of educating privately in Athens—had reported him becoming ambivalent about his lessons and withdrawing more into himself. 'She has come to stay with us.'

Loukas didn't answer, just stared at Xander with his big blue eyes.

'Will you say hello to her?'

Loukas shook his head, his thick mop of blond hair falling into his eyes. It needed cutting, Xander thought, his heart aching to see the emptiness in his nephew's eyes.

It was at moments like this he wanted to grab his brother by the throat and shake him for all the crap he'd put his son through.

He knew Yanis and Katerina couldn't help their addictions. He'd read all the literature and spoken to all the specialists; they all said the same thing. And in fairness to his brother and sister-in-law, they'd done their best to protect Loukas from it all. In their pitiful marriage they had at least tried to do the right thing by him, but they hadn't accounted for their son being like a sponge and taking it all in: the regular hospitalisations, the frequent disappearing acts, the rows when the pain of their marriage broke through the alcohol and drug-inflicted stupors.

The best thing would be for them to divorce. They should never have married in the first place.

He did his best to understand them. The greatest emotion he felt towards them was pity but he could gladly shout himself hoarse to tell them that their best wasn't good enough and that their son deserved better. But they already knew that.

Taking Loukas's hand in his, Xander smiled. 'Elizabeth is a nice lady. I promise. Maybe you can talk to her later. Would you like that?'

Loukas shook his head.

He could sense Elizabeth flinching behind him.

'Can we have breakfast? I've been waiting for you,' Loukas whispered in Greek. 'We've set the table in the infinity room.'

'Nai.' Yes.

'Not you.' Loukas's eyes suddenly fixed on Elizabeth. He'd rediscovered his English. 'You go away.'

Elizabeth felt as if she'd been struck.

The little boy's intense gaze didn't leave her face, as if he thought he could make her disappear with the force of his will.

'Loukas, that isn't a polite thing to say to our guest, is it?' Xander said in a low tone. 'You must say sorry to her.'

To her horror, a tear appeared in Loukas's left eye and fell down his face. His little shoulders heaved and this time a torrent of tears fell. Xander gathered him into his arms and carefully stood, Loukas clinging to him, his face buried in his neck.

Murmuring soothing words in Greek to his nephew, Xander threw an apologetic look at Elizabeth before indicating that she should follow them.

She walked behind them through an enormous living area, then through to a second cavernous room with a rounded ceiling. A dining table had been laid by a far wall. Xander set Loukas down and brushed away the last of his tears with his thumb, then took the seat next to him.

Feeling as awkward as she'd ever done in her life, Elizabeth sat herself opposite Loukas, Xander sitting between them at the head of the table. She barely registered the infinity pool just feet from them pouring out into a wall-less expanse that looked out over the Aegean, too overwhelmed at the situation to be overawed by anything like such an ostentatious display of wealth.

More staff appeared, carrying trays of yogurt and honey, fresh fruit, pastries and coffee.

Loukas shuffled his chair as close to his uncle as he could get, clearly thrilled to have him back. More than thrilled, she came to think later. Enthralled.

As she watched uncle and nephew interact, she understood why Xander had been so resolute in keeping his promise in returning to him. Xander was clearly Loukas's hero.

When they'd finished eating and the plates had been cleared, a woman who was introduced as Loukas's English nanny came in.

'It's time to get dressed,' she told her charge. 'We're meeting Alekos soon to make dens.'

He pulled a mutinous face. 'I don't want to go.'

'You wanted to the other day. Come on.'

Loukas looked hopefully at his uncle. 'Can you come with me?'

Xander ruffled his hair. 'We've had a long flight and need to rest. We'll do something fun when you get back. Does that sound good?'

His chin wobbling, his nephew nodded and got down from the table.

Throughout their breakfast he hadn't looked at Elizabeth once.

CHAPTER SIX

XANDER POURED HIMSELF another cup of coffee then moved to fill Elizabeth's. She put a hand over her cup.

'I think my brain might explode if I have any more caffeine.'

He knew the feeling. He was struggling to keep his eyes open himself.

'I apologise for Loukas's behaviour,' he said.

She gave a rueful smile. 'He's protective of you, that's all. He's vulnerable. With his parents both absent, you're his security.' She paused before asking, 'Is he used to seeing you with women?'

'God, no.' He'd always been comfortable entertaining women in Athens but Diadonus was his home, a place to live and entertain family and close friends, not the socialites who littered his world. If he brought a lover here they might start getting ideas that he wanted to make the affair permanent.

Xander conducted his relationships in the same way Elizabeth matched her clients, without lies or deceit. Straight down the line. He didn't want marriage and he made damned sure any lover knew it.

He'd done marriage once with Elizabeth but that had been a whole combination of elements thinking for him, mostly his libido, most definitely not his brain.

In those dark awful days of dealing with Ana's death, Elizabeth's tears still fresh in his mind, he'd known he would never marry again. He didn't need it or want it, or the misery and contempt that accompanied every marriage he knew.

He didn't know a single couple who'd found lasting happiness together. Quite the opposite.

Strangely, his parents had the most content marriage he knew, if *content* was the right word, but they were incredibly well-suited, narcissists the pair of them.

Elizabeth's cheeks coloured and she looked away, tucking a strand of honey-blonde hair behind her ear. 'He's probably scared I'm going to take you away from him. Does he know where his parents are?'

'He knows his mother's in hospital. He thinks Yanis is away on business.'

'Has he seen Katerina since she was hospitalised?'

'A couple of times.' Noticing how wiped out Elizabeth looked, he finished his coffee and got to his feet. 'I'll show you around.'

Elizabeth followed him out of the cave-like living area she'd been told was known as the infinity room, and into the proper living area that was fully protected from the elements. From there she was shown the main dining room, study, playroom with a full-sized snooker table, and kitchen. The sense of space was everywhere and, despite all the futuristic gizmos and gadgets, the design of the villa itself was sympathetic to the island's heritage.

'Did you design this yourself?' she asked.

'I worked closely with the architect on the blue-prints but I can't take credit for it.'

Then he took her down a flight of extraordinarily wide stairs to the ground floor. There were seven bedrooms in all, each with their own bathroom. They passed a room with the door open. It was a young boy's bedroom. Muffled voices came from it.

'Does Loukas have his own bedroom here?' she whispered.

Xander nodded grimly and matched her low tone. 'He's stayed with me regularly since he was born but in recent years it's become a lot more frequent. When I had the house built I let him choose his own furnishings and decoration for his room. He knows he'll always have a home here.'

'Does he have a bedroom at your parents' place too?'

'He's never spent a night with them and he never will,' he answered with such venom that Elizabeth took a wary step back.

'If you hate your parents so much, how can you work with them? Or have I got that wrong?'

'I wouldn't go as far as to say I hate them,' he said.

'But you do still work together?'

'Of course.'

'How does that work with you being at war over Loukas?'

'That's personal. Work is business. We're very adept at separating the two.'

And she thought *her* family was dysfunctional.

'So you don't have *any* issue working with them? You've never been tempted to sack them? I read that right; you *are* the boss?'

'Yes, I'm the boss, but why would I? They're both excellent in their respective roles within the company. It's only as human beings that they're useless.'

This was too much for Elizabeth to get her head around. She'd surrounded herself with a workforce of warm, decent people. She'd never even contemplated employing someone she didn't like, once passing over a multilingual secretary who would've been able to translate contracts into six different languages. She'd preferred the one who could only translate three because she'd been a warmer person.

She'd had her fill of cold people growing up.

'I need to get some sleep before I do any more work,' she said, wanting nothing more than to be alone. So much had happened in the past twenty-four hours she felt dizzy. 'Which one's my room?'

'We're at the end of the floor.' He set off towards it.

'Adjoining rooms?' she clarified, only following him when he nodded. 'And there's a lock?'

'Correct. Worry not, *kardia mou*, your virtue is safe with me.' But as he spoke a flash of heat pulsed from his eyes, quickly gone but there long enough to make her heart ripple.

He looked away to put his hand on the handle of

her door. 'Spend the day resting. Tomorrow we'll go to Athens.'

'What for?'

'You need clothes, don't you?'

'Doesn't Diadonus have shops?'

'Not the sort of clothes a wife of mine should wear. I don't care what style of clothing you buy but I do care about the label on the back.'

She nodded, understanding. Image was important in this world. To some people, image was everything. If she was to be Xander's wife, she had to look the part and that meant couture clothing.

What did she mean, *if she was to be* his wife? She already *was* his wife.

The thought sent a little jolt through her and, for the first time, it really hit her. Xander was her husband. Her legally married husband.

And, for the first time, she allowed herself to see the memory she had shoved in a tight box in the furthest recess of her mind. What it had been like to make love to him as his wife. How it had felt to have him inside her, a part of her...

Long-forgotten heat coiled through her loins at the memories, burning into her brain...

A long, long silence stretched out between them, the atmosphere thickening until Xander's jaw clenched and he shoved the door open. He spoke brusquely. 'This is your room. Make yourself at home. If you need anything you'll find a member of staff in the kitchen.'

She practically dived into it, shutting the door

firmly behind her without exchanging another word, desperate to be away from him.

Alone in the pretty room that would put the world's finest hotels to shame, she clutched at her cheeks.

It was the lack of sleep causing her thoughts and emotions to veer so wildly, she assured herself. It was no wonder old memories were being dredged up. A good night's sleep and some distance from Xander would put her back on an even keel.

She tried the internal doors. She opened three before she found the one adjoining Xander's room. It was already locked on the other side.

'Have you been to Athens before?' Xander asked her the next day, shortly before they were due to land. 'Other than just the airport?'

'A handful of times, but that was work. I don't know the city at all.' She was dressed in the clothing she'd worn out to St Francis, his staff having laundered it for her overnight. Her honey-blonde hair was loose and glossy around her shoulders, all signs of exhaustion from the day before eradicated.

They'd managed to avoid each other for the rest of the day, Elizabeth staying in her room, only emerging at dinner. She'd eaten quickly, making only the blandest of conversation before excusing herself, her goodnight to Loukas going unacknowledged.

They'd breakfasted early and dropped Loukas at school on their way to the airstrip. He had refused to look at Elizabeth. He hadn't spoken to her since he'd told her to go away. Xander knew the best thing he could do was give his nephew time to get used to her being there.

He handed her a credit card.

'What's this for?'

'To pay for your clothes and other stuff. There's no limit on it so spend whatever you like.'

She looked momentarily disconcerted but then nodded and slipped it into her purse.

'You don't feel comfortable taking it?'

'I've paid my own way for ten years. It's a little strange, that's all, but I know it's necessary. I can't afford to buy a new expensive wardrobe with what's in my bank account. The money you've paid me won't last long once I've refunded all my clients.'

'Give me a list of the refunds and I'll reimburse you.' He should have thought about that before.

'Okay.' She shrugged. 'And I'll give you my shopping receipts later so you can deduct it from the final amount you pay me when this is all over.'

'There will be no deductions. While you're acting as my wife I'll pick up all your tabs. The money I'm giving you is recompense for the loss of your business.'

But they weren't acting, he reminded himself. Elizabeth really *was* his wife. And as he thought this, she met his gaze. A look passed between them, one that sent heat to his loins and the faintest hint of colour to her cheeks.

Xander gritted his teeth and turned away to look out of the window.

When he'd first learned their annulment hadn't gone through, the thought of her being his wife had been an abstract concept. It hadn't seemed in the slightest bit real. Their marriage was a piece of paper, nothing more.

Two days together, back with the one woman in the world who'd been able to turn his head as well as his loins, and that piece of paper was starting to feel a lot different.

He didn't deny that he'd once had real feelings for Elizabeth but that had been the result of the chemistry neither had felt restrained from acting upon. So strong had it been that it was hardly surprising remnants of it still simmered between them.

How would she react if he grabbed her to him and kissed her?

Locking his jaw, he wiped the pointless question from his mind.

Whatever desire Elizabeth might feel for him now, she'd made it clear she wouldn't entertain acting upon it. And neither would he. She might not be the dreamer from before but he'd given his word and intended to keep it.

The adjoining door separating their two bedrooms would remain locked for the duration of their marriage.

Elizabeth's few visits to Athens had left an impression in her head of a bustling city brimming with noisy, exuberant people. Those impressions turned out to be correct. Athens was an *amazing* city.

Xander got his driver to drop her in the Kolonaki district where, he assured her, she would have no trouble finding suitable shops to buy a new closet of clothes in.

Being an enthusiastic shopper, she welcomed the opportunity to forget her troubles for a few hours of retail therapy. That she didn't have to consider price tags made for a welcome bonus.

Living in New York was expensive. Her mortgage payments took a huge chunk of her income so she normally selected her clothing carefully, knowing she had to choose items that made her look professional but not threatening. She had to fit into whoever's company she might find herself and, most of all, she had to not stand out. She had to be unobtrusive. Most of all, what she selected had to be affordable.

Suddenly, she could dress for herself again, something she hadn't felt able to do since she'd left college and formed Leviathan.

About to hand her new credit card over to an assistant in a boutique that sold the most gorgeous clothes, she felt her cell vibrate through her purse and pulled it out. It was a message from Xander telling her to make sure to buy herself some evening wear.

Her cheeks heated at the words. Evening wear…? Then she realised he meant cocktail dresses and gowns, not lingerie.

Turning her mind away from wearing anything racy in front of Xander, she paid for her goods, which were boxed up for her and put aside for Xander's driver to collect later, and walked to an upmarket department store further up the street. She might have no intention of buying anything racy but she did need to buy underwear.

After five hours she'd spent an absolute fortune and wandered to Kolonaki Square to find the café she'd agreed to meet Xander at.

Her heart skipped to find him already there, chatting on his phone. He'd removed his tie and undone the top button of his shirt.

When he spotted her, he ended his call and stood to greet her.

'Are you done?' he asked, putting his hands on her hips and pressing a kiss to her lips.

The gesture was so unexpected that she froze.

Xander had *kissed* her.

He gave a half-smile and traced a thumb across her jawline. 'Married couples usually kiss, *kardia mou*.'

Totally flustered, she groped for the nearest chair to sit on. 'Can't we just settle on air kisses?'

His eyes held hers. 'Not in public. Take a seat. I've ordered us coffee.'

She put her purse on the table and opened the menu. 'I'm starving. Have we got time for me to grab a salad?'

'We've plenty of time.'

She scanned the menu, anything but to have to look at him. Looking at Xander made her stomach do funny things. It made her entire body do funny things.

When a waitress arrived with their coffee she ordered a slice of chocolate baklava tart.

Xander pulled a bemused face at her choice. 'I thought you were going to have a salad?'

'So did I until I saw the word chocolate.'

He grinned and there, right before her eyes, he turned into the young man with the irresistible smile she'd fallen in love with all those years ago.

Her heart, already pounding erratically, seemed to bloom within her chest and an ache spread low in her belly. She had to fight to stop herself staring at the exposed strong throat and the sensuous lips she had so loved to kiss.

'Is something the matter?' he asked, staring at her closely.

She grabbed her coffee, but as she shook her head to deny anything was wrong a sense of dread raced through her to realise that, as incomprehensible as it was, she wanted him to do far more than kiss her.

Xander checked his watch as he waited for Elizabeth to appear. He'd had to leave early that morning for a breakfast meeting in Athens and only just made it back in time to say goodnight to Loukas.

He hadn't seen her all day. That hadn't stopped him from constantly thinking about her, which was damned frustrating as he was supposed to be concentrating on spreadsheets for the company's year end.

He took satisfaction from the fact that their profits for the year were up seven per cent, but with his head in Diadonus and the woman living under his roof that satisfaction was muted.

His thoughts were broken when a figure stepped into the infinity room.

The effect was like being struck by a bat. 'Elizabeth?'

'You sound surprised,' she said tartly. 'You summoned me and here I am.'

He'd messaged her earlier to say they would be eating out that night.

'Your hair…'

Unlike the glossy sleek hair he'd become accustomed to, she'd gone for the natural look, drying it into a mass of thick, tight blonde curls.

'What's wrong with it?' she demanded.

'Nothing. It's beautiful.' He'd forgotten how curly her hair truly was. The difference was astounding.

Looking at her…

It was like staring at a portrait of the past and he had to swallow a lump in his throat that accompanied the sudden strong hammer of his heart.

The insolence that had been set on her face when she entered the room softened and colour stained her cheeks as she looked away from him and murmured, 'It takes for ever to straighten.'

'Why do it, then?'

A shrug. 'It made me feel more professional. And now I don't need to look professional, so…' Another shrug.

She was wearing a pretty baby-pink dress that fell below her knees and had the thinnest of straps, falling in a V to skim her golden cleavage.

He remembered the first time he'd taken one of

her breasts into his mouth. He'd thought nature must have made them especially for him. Small but beautifully formed, enough to fit into his mouth and cover with the palm of his hand. He remembered making love to her, how she would arch her back and grab his hair, how her legs would tighten around him as she came with loud moans.

Suddenly he ached to have her, to thrust deep inside her and experience that heady pleasure again.

He'd never found that compatibility or connection with anyone else. He'd had relationships throughout the years but had always been careful in his selection of lovers. No wide-eyed dreamers with a zest for life. No one with the potential to charm him with one beaming smile or a ringing laugh. Not that there was anyone remotely like her in his world.

A decade ago she'd been a virgin. He'd been old enough to have experience but young enough to still be discovering women's bodies. By the end of their fortnight together he knew more about the workings of Elizabeth's body than he knew of his own.

Making love to her now would be different from how it had been ten years ago. They both had an adulthood of experience to add into what was already proving to be a combustible mix.

'Let's make a move,' he said abruptly. *Theos*, he couldn't be alone in a room with her for a minute without thinking of sex.

She wrapped a creamy shawl around her shoulders. 'Where are we going?'

'Diadonus Town.'

Her relief was obvious.

'What?'

'I thought you were going to take me to Athens.'

'You don't like Athens?'

'Sure, but it's a bit of a pain to get to if we're only going for a meal.'

That those were his exact thoughts was something he kept to himself.

'Just so you're prepared, there's a few members of the press on the island itching to get another picture of us together, so remember to smile.'

'I shall turn my frown upside down.'

With a tug in his groin, he was taken by the urge to wipe the frown off her face with something stronger than words.

Jamming his hands in his pockets, he led the way out.

The restaurant Xander took her to was a short drive away, an old-fashioned *taverna* perched above a beach. There were only six other diners.

'Is it always this quiet?' Elizabeth asked while they waited for the main courses to be served.

'It's winter,' he answered with a shrug. 'Come the spring and the whole of Diadonus will be filled with tourists.'

'I read it's a party island.'

'We attract a young crowd but it's not like Mykonos or Santorini. We get a lot of family vacationers.'

'Do the tourists bother you?'

'Not at all. Tourists are what keeps our economy floating.'

She sipped her glass of rosé and was relieved when the owner returned to their table with their next course. If they were eating she could pretend the atmosphere between them didn't shimmer with a strange electricity and that every time she met his gaze her lower belly didn't clench with longing.

CHAPTER SEVEN

FOR THE FIRST TIME in days, Elizabeth finished a meal. A couple Xander knew had joined them for a few minutes to say hello, which had given her time to regroup mentally. They hadn't spoken English so the only requirement on Elizabeth's part had been to smile and not flinch when Xander took possessive control of her hand. Having his warm skin against hers...

She could still feel the tingles in her bloodstream.

Now they were alone again, she pushed her empty plate to one side and gazed out across the sandy beach, drinking the view in. Diadonus was more beautiful than she had imagined. 'Why did you go to St Francis for a vacation when you live in your own paradise?'

Xander took so long to answer that she thought he was ignoring her.

'Going to St Francis, it wasn't a vacation, it was an escape,' he eventually said.

'Why?'

His eyes met hers. 'I didn't want to stick around for the fallout when I ended my engagement to Ana.'

'You ran away?'

'That's one way of looking at it,' he conceded.

Looking back, Xander could see he had taken the coward's way out. It hadn't seemed like that at the time of course. To his twenty-year-old self it had seemed perfectly logical. If he took himself off, there would be no one in his ear demanding he change his mind. He'd determined to go back when the dust had settled but in the interim take some time out and see something of the world that wasn't business related. Have some fun like others of his age.

In his arrogance it hadn't crossed his mind that Ana would have to suffer the price of his absence.

'How long after you ended your engagement did you leave?'

'Two days.'

'You didn't even give me two hours.' She shook her head, her long curls bobbing with the motion.

'There was no point in prolonging it for either of us.'

'For either of us?' There was a catch in her voice. 'That makes it sound like you cared for me.'

'I *did* care for you, Elizabeth.'

Her eyes flashed. 'Did you care for Ana too? Did you tell her you loved her and that you couldn't live without her like you told me?'

He took a long drink of his beer, studying the tight-set face before him. He remembered saying those words to Elizabeth. He remembered meaning them.

'My relationship with Ana was nothing like the one between you and me.'

'Of course it wasn't. She was your childhood sweetheart.'

'We were *never* childhood sweethearts. We mixed in the same circles, we were casual friends, but that was the extent of it. We got engaged when I turned twenty because it was expected of us and our parents made it very clear it was what they wanted. It's traditional in my family to marry young and with someone who can bring wealth and contacts to the family business. My father married my mother because she was an heiress. Their marriage was arranged by their own parents. My brother married Katerina for the same reason. Ana came from an extremely rich family from Mykonos. We were engaged for less than a month.'

'If you were so well-suited, why did you end it?'

'Because it wasn't what I wanted and I should never have gone along with it.' He should have trusted his gut instincts from the start. Instead, he'd let his misgivings fester until they'd become bugs hatching in his skin.

Elizabeth's expression remained stony.

'I wasn't in love with her. I didn't want to be trapped in a marriage I couldn't get out of like Yanis was. Divorce is unheard of in my family. It's too risky for the business. From what Yanis tells me, they haven't had sex since they conceived Loukas. Even before that it was a volatile relationship.' He drained his beer. 'I decided that no marriage was better than living with one like theirs.'

'Yanis wanted out even then?'

'They both did. I'm certain it's why they turned to drugs and alcohol. It numbed it for them.' He paused before adding, 'They were both in love with other people.'

Her eyebrows drew together. 'So why did they go along with the marriage in the first place?'

'The alternative meant being cut off.'

'Weren't you worried that would happen to you when you dumped Ana?'

He grimaced at her bluntly delivered words. 'For sure, but I've always been more independently minded than Yanis. I took an educated risk. Yanis has never had much input in the business but I'd already proven myself to be an asset. I knew my decision would enrage my parents but they're clever people and clever people do not cast off assets making them money.'

But they hadn't been so clever when Xander had made the deal that resulted in Timos SE being signed under his control, taking the power and control away from them for ever.

Elizabeth was silent before asking, 'How did Ana take it?'

Xander signalled for another beer. 'Better than I thought she would. I thought she was okay with it. For sure, I knew she would be a little hurt; everyone's got their pride, but she understood. She was a nice girl. Better than most of the socialites I grew up with who were so vapid they made a plastic doll seem like a Nobel laureate.'

Ana really *had* been nice. She'd been sweet and warm, a woman any right-thinking man in his position would have been proud to call his wife. It hadn't been her fault he'd felt zero desire towards her.

His parents had both openly taken lovers through the years but that hadn't been something he could entertain. To Xander, marriage meant fidelity and commitment otherwise why do it? If he'd had to marry anyone it would be someone he desired and who held his intellectual interest too. He'd been selfish. He'd wanted it all. And so he'd ended it with Ana, determined that he *would* have it all.

Then he'd met Elizabeth and had known for certain he'd made the right choice. In his continued arrogance he'd married her without taking into account how utterly unsuited she was to a life as his wife.

His fresh beer was brought over. He took it straight from the waiter's hand and took a large swig of it.

Talking about Ana, thinking about Ana, was *hard*, talking about her to Elizabeth, who he'd also hurt, doubly so. It brought it all back: all the rancid guilt that lived inside him. Ana would never marry. She would never have children.

He forced the rest of the story out. 'Two weeks after I ended it she crashed her car into a tree. She wasn't much of a drinker but she'd drunk heavily that night. I have no idea if she intended to kill herself or not.'

Elizabeth didn't say anything, just stared at him with a stunned expression on her face. He searched for the condemnation he knew he deserved but couldn't interpret what came from her eyes.

'Her family...even though I told *everyone* that she was blameless, they blamed her for not doing enough to keep me. I didn't know it at the time. Yanis filled me in when I got home. They put pressure on her. My parents got in on the act too. They all told her I would come to my senses and that she would have to change to keep me. But she knew I wouldn't change my mind. She knew the situation was hopeless but I was oblivious to it all, thousands of miles away in a Caribbean paradise, all my problems forgotten about because I was with you.'

'You don't blame yourself, surely?' she asked with sudden animation.

'If I hadn't abandoned her to deal with the fallout of the break-up alone, she would be alive today, of that I am certain.' He shook his head, self-loathing filling him. Talking of Ana's death made his guts feel they were being eaten without anaesthetic.

Elizabeth's eyes held his for the longest time, the gold and red flecks shining. 'If anyone's to blame it's her family and your parents for treating her like a commodity.'

He'd known that ever since Yanis told him of the pressure they'd all put her under, but that didn't change his own responsibility.

He'd left Ana to deal with the fallout on her own, in his arrogance assuming that because he was all right then she would be too. It hadn't occurred to him that their families would turn on her. He should have protected her.

At least he'd been able to protect Elizabeth from his family, however badly it had hurt her at the time.

'And, Xander, you can't know what was going through her head or what other influences might have been in play when she got behind the wheel.'

'Whatever was going on in her head wasn't good.'

'The outcome might have been the same even if you hadn't broken the engagement.'

What a tragic waste of a life, Elizabeth thought, her heart aching for the young Greek woman. A tiny part of her heart also ached for Xander bearing the weight of such guilt. She could see it in his eyes.

He held her gaze for an age before his eyes snapped back into focus and he said in a measured voice, 'So there it is. You know it all. My world is a beautiful place to live in but a cruel place to be. Think yourself lucky that in a few months you'll be able to leave it.'

She finished her wine and gazed back out at the foamy surf, a deep ache spreading out from her chest.

'Do you want dessert?' he asked.

'No, thank you.'

He reached for his phone. 'I'll get my driver to collect us.'

She stared with more longing at the sandy shore. 'If we walked along the beach, would it take us to your villa?'

'Yes but it's a couple of miles.'

'I think I'll do that. I need to walk.' Walking was good. It always cleared her head and made sense of whatever madness she was living in. Right then, she had so many thoughts racing through her it would take a marathon to clear it.

She could sense his surprise. 'Okay. Give me a minute to settle the bill and we'll get going.'

To reach the beach from the restaurant involved descending a steep incline with only the moonlight to guide them. Inhaling the air that reminded her so heavily of St Francis it made her heart clench and twist. Biting the swirling emotions back, Elizabeth removed her heels and navigated her way carefully down the incline until she felt cool sand between her toes.

The night sea was making its familiar lapping noise. She remembered how soothing she'd found the sound on her first trip to St Francis, her first trip to any beach. *Everything* on St Francis had been soothing. Except it had all been an illusion. The serenity had created an ambiance that had lulled her into believing things that weren't real. Here, on Diadonus, there were different scents, equally beautiful, but without the muscle memory reactions.

Would she one day inhale a scent and be taken back to this moment in time?

At least if that happened the memories wouldn't lance her.

There was a gentle breeze coming from the sea and she wrapped her shawl around her shoulders and walked right to the water's edge. She prodded a toe into it but the surf was too cold and she stepped back, right in time for a gentle wave to cover her foot.

Needing to move, she set off, treading footprints into the wet sand that were eradicated almost immediately by the waves. Just as their marriage had been eradicated almost immediately after exchanging their vows.

'If divorce is too risky for your business, how can you risk divorcing me?' she asked quietly.

'You haven't brought any assets into the marriage. There's no contract between us. I can pay you off and that's it. Over with.'

'And when we finally are over with? Will you ever marry again?'

'No.' The word was blunt. 'I know of no marriages that last without turning to hell. I would be left with the choice of living with someone I dislike or risk destroying my company with a bitter divorce.'

Elizabeth knew exactly how vicious divorces could be. And while he wasn't saying anything she didn't agree with, it still made her heart twinge.

'What about children?' she forced herself to ask, glad she didn't have to see his expression when he gave his answer. He was walking beside her, his hands deep in his pockets, a foot apart but close enough that her senses danced with awareness.

It had always been like this. She'd only needed to catch a glimpse of him to feel every atom of her body vibrate.

'Don't you want to produce the next generation of Trakases?'

'Loukas is the next generation.'

'But don't you want your own?' she persisted. He had once. Or had that been a lie too?

'Children need two parents. I'm never going to marry again so for me it's not a consideration.'

'What if Loukas doesn't want to join the business?'

'That's for him to decide when he's old enough. While I'm alive and kicking I shall run it the best way I can and put the structures in place for it to thrive when I'm gone.'

There was nothing she could say to that. And what did it matter to her in any case? They would go their separate ways soon enough and then she'd never have to see him again.

They were approaching a harbour. A row of yachts of varying sizes lay before them, pearlescent under the moonlight.

She remembered the day Xander had chartered a yacht for them. It was the first time she'd really considered that he must come from money, his familiarity with sailing and the unwritten protocols...

It should have been a warning sign. Instead it had delighted her. In her head she'd already moved to Diadonus to be with him. They wouldn't starve while she completed her degree, learnt his language and found a job.

Her blood burned and her heart ached to remember her innocence. Voices called out in her head, happy memories that had turned into scars.

'I seem to remember you never liked walking,' he said, breaking the rolling silence that had formed between them.

She tried not to flinch. It was hard to hold on to her loathing of him when he so casually dropped in things she'd expected him to have forgotten.

She was finding it hard to hold on to her loathing period.

'I learned to like walking when I enrolled at New York State. After rent and tuition were paid I was stony broke. To save money I walked everywhere. I still do.'

'Why did you quit Brown?'

After the confidences he'd shared over their meal it seemed petty not to answer him. 'My mother withdrew her funding so I had no choice.'

'Why did she do that?'

'I told her I didn't want to major in English any more.'

She could feel his eyes burning into her.

'Why on earth would you do that? You'd only ever wanted to be a writer.'

'I did,' she agreed, wishing her heart didn't twist to remember the person she'd been then. 'I wanted to write scripts for films about modern-day love; stories with hints of the classics running through them, but when I returned home to New York the idea of writing *anything* about love was laughable. There was no way I could write about something I didn't believe in any more, and script writing? Every girl in my class and her cat wanted to do that. I decided to go into business instead. I had no idea at the time what kind of business I wanted, but I knew I would be my own boss. My mother had other ideas, so I decided to go it alone.'

'Why would she not want you to go into business?'

'The only thing my mom has ever taken pride in about me were my achievements in English. I was winning literature prizes when I was eight and a career in writing was a foregone conclusion. When I told her I wanted to major in business…' She took a deep breath, hating the memories. It felt like a different life. 'The long and short of it was that if I refused to major in English, she would stop supporting me.'

'So you moved out and transferred colleges off your own back?'

She wrapped her shawl tighter around her. The breeze had picked up, the chill now setting goosebumps off on her flesh. 'I was legally an adult. She couldn't force me to do anything. No one could. I still had some of the money granny had left me. It wasn't enough to support me at Brown but was enough to pay for the first year's tuition and rent at New York State, which was my home college. So I moved out of my mom's and transferred there.'

'Your father couldn't help you?'

'Nope. He'd just remarried a woman equally as manipulative as my mother. After a decade of war

with my mom he was tired of arguing with women—
that's what he told me, anyway.' She speared him
with a look. 'So you don't have the monopoly on
dysfunctional, emotionally abusive parents.'

'I'm beginning to see that,' he said after a long
pause.

Somehow during their walk, their pace had
slowed and the distance between them closed. Xander's arm brushed lightly against hers.

The heat that rushed through her...

Her lungs seemed to close in on themselves.

'No wonder you forgot to chase our annulment
with all that going on,' he murmured.

She forced herself to concentrate on the conversation at hand, not on the warm body brushing against
her own, and moved out of his way so they were no
longer touching.

The chill felt starker without his heat warming
her.

'The annulment was the last thing on my mind,'
she croaked. 'I never even thought there might be a
problem with it.'

Xander's villa appeared shortly ahead of them.
As they got closer, they drifted together again, close
enough that if she flexed her fingers she'd be able
to touch him.

In silence they passed the barrier onto his private
section of beach, security lights bathing them the
moment they stepped onto his land.

Her heart rate increasing so much she no longer
felt the individual beats, Elizabeth hurried up the

steps to enter the villa from the kitchen. She didn't know the entry code.

She moved back down to allow him to get to it but the steps were narrow and it turned into an awkward kind of dance as they tried to step around each other.

And then, without knowing how, she found herself trapped between the railing and Xander.

Her breath caught in a throat that had filled with moisture. Unable to help herself, she tilted her head to gaze into eyes that trapped her more effectively than any chain could. The few senses not already on high alert sprang to life, lips tingling, every cell in her body straining towards him.

The look in his eyes…it was as if he wanted to eat her whole.

His mouth drifted slowly to hers, his eyes open and holding hers in their hypnotic gaze until the lids closed and she felt his warm breath brush against her skin in the moment before his mouth found hers.

For the longest time they didn't move, their lips only whispering against the other's.

He pulled back a little to stare at her again, and the hunger in his eyes darkened and he wrapped his arms around her to crush her to him.

Their lips fused together in a kiss full of such passion that her bones melted and then *she* melted, right into him, her hands grasping round to hold onto his back, crushing herself to *him*.

As their tongues danced together and the heat of his mouth consumed her, she clung even tighter, dizzy with the familiarity of his taste and the terrifying yet exhilarating familiarity of her own responses.

His hands burrowed into her hair and she wanted to cry as she remembered how he had done the exact same thing the first time he'd kissed her all those years ago.

If the kitchen door hadn't burst open at that moment, there was every chance she would have lost herself completely.

'So this is what you get up to when you're supposed to be caring for my grandson.'

Elizabeth let go of Xander as sharply as if she'd had ice tipped over her.

Standing in the doorway, as tall and menacing as Morticia Adams with all her hair chopped off, stood a woman she could only presume was Xander's mother.

CHAPTER EIGHT

XANDER REGAINED HIS composure before she did. He straightened and shook his head, and brushed past his mother.

'How did you get in?'

'I knocked and the door was answered. Your housekeeper told me you were out. I said I would wait.'

Listening to her, Elizabeth revised her opinion of Morticia Adams to one of Marlene Dietrich but with less of an accent. Her English was, like her son's, impeccable. As was her timing.

Hastily straightening her dress, Elizabeth grabbed her shawl that had fallen to the ground and, her head reeling, her legs weakened, her body vibrating from the effect of his kiss, she followed them inside.

She didn't know what she was most mortified about: that she'd fallen into Xander's arms so easily or that his mother's first impression of her would be her kissing her son so passionately.

She could get down on her knees in gratitude that she'd interrupted them before it had gone any further.

As skinny as a pencil, Mirela Trakas had cropped jet-black hair and the surprised face of someone on first-name terms with her plastic surgeon. Wearing a black pantsuit with full make-up and a dozen solid gold bangles hanging on her wrists, she strongly resembled a glamourous undertaker.

'If you'd called first I would have told you not to bother,' Xander said.

'That's why I didn't call first. I'll have a gin and tonic.'

A grim smile on his handsome face, he strode through the kitchen and dining room and into the infinity room, where he kept a wall-length bar. 'I thought you were in Milan.'

'We wrapped up early, so I thought I'd call in on my favourite son.'

The look Xander gave her perfectly conveyed his feelings. Nostrils flaring, he said, 'Dad not with you?'

'He's gone to Monte Carlo for the evening to gamble your inheritance at the roulette table.'

Xander rolled his eyes. 'I assume Elizabeth's the reason you're here?'

'Elizabeth? Is that her name?'

'You know perfectly well it is. Elizabeth, meet my mother. Mirela, meet your new daughter-in-law.'

Mirela didn't even glance in Elizabeth's direction. 'It would have been nice to learn my son had married from the son in question rather than hear about it third-hand. My phone has been ringing off the hook. All my friends know about it. The whole world knows about it. Even nuns in Outer Mongolia know about it but you couldn't take the time to tell me.'

'We've been busy.'

'So I see.' Her nostrils flared in an exact replica of her son's. 'You tell the judge you want guardianship of my grandson yet leave him with strangers to take your fake wife out. I'm sure the judge will be thrilled when I share it with him next week.'

He poured himself a large Scotch and downed it in one. Feeling as if she needed something strong too, Elizabeth stood beside him and poured herself one, downing it the same as he'd done.

Oh, wow. Her throat *burned*. And Mirela noticed, wicked pleasure alive in her cold eyes.

Thrusting a gin and tonic into his mother's hand, Xander contemplated her coolly before saying, 'Loukas is in bed asleep. He's being watched by people he's known his entire life, and who love him. Rather like you and Dad would leave Yanis and I alone while you two went out which, if I'm remembering correctly, was every night. You also left us alone for weeks at a time...'

'That was always business, darling.'

'That week in the Maldives was not business. Nor the frequent skiing trips to Canada. I could drink this whole bottle of single malt and I'd still be listing the times you and Dad took off without us that had nothing to do with business.'

Mirela waved her hand. 'The Maldives would have bored you.'

'Yes, you told us that when you got back after not

FREE Merchandise is 'in the Cards' for you!

Dear Reader,

We're giving away FREE MERCHANDISE!

Seriously, we'd like to reward you for reading this novel by giving you **FREE MERCHANDISE** worth over $20 retail. And no purchase is necessary!

You see the Jack of Hearts sticker above? Paste that sticker in the box on the Free Merchandise Voucher inside. Return the Voucher today... and we'll send you Free Merchandise!

Thanks again for reading one of our novels—and enjoy your Free Merchandise with our compliments!

Pam Powers

Pam Powers

P.S. Look inside to see what Free Merchandise is **"in the cards"** for you!

BUSINESS REPLY MAIL

FIRST-CLASS MAIL   PERMIT NO. 717   BUFFALO, NY

POSTAGE WILL BE PAID BY ADDRESSEE

READER SERVICE

PO BOX 1867

BUFFALO NY 14240-9952

NO POSTAGE
NECESSARY
IF MAILED
IN THE
UNITED STATES

bothering to tell us you were going in the first place. We had to find out from the staff.'

'We couldn't have been expected to report our every movement to our *children*. We had a multimillion-euro business to run and the staff were perfectly well placed to look after you.' She laughed and took a good sip of her drink.

'You could have done and you should have done. That multimillion-euro business has turned into a multibillion business since I've been at the helm and I'm still able to eat breakfast every day with Loukas when he's in my care. His future is all that matters and that future does not include you being his guardian, so finish your drink and get out.'

She pouted. Elizabeth would have laughed if she weren't so appalled. Mirela had actually *pouted*.

'You're kicking me out when I still haven't spoken properly to my new daughter-in-law?' Mirela's beady eyes finally fixed upon her. 'Or should that be *old* daughter-in-law?'

Was that a dig at her age or that they'd been unwittingly married for a decade?

'You're not pregnant already, are you, darling? Or do you just like your food?'

'When I get pregnant you'll be the first to know,' Elizabeth said, ignoring the barb. She held out a hand. 'It's been a pleasure meeting you... Do I call you Mother?'

Mirela looked at the extended hand and then surprised Elizabeth by shaking it. Before she released it, she studied it a moment then said, 'I know a good manicurist in Athens. I'll get the number passed on to you. And I know just the place you can get a chemical peel for your acne scars.'

If Elizabeth had acne scars she might have been offended. As she didn't, she did the only thing she could think of. She laughed. 'I can see exactly why Xander and Yanis don't want you anywhere near Loukas.'

'And I can see exactly why Xander kept you a secret for ten years,' Mirela shot back. She opened her mouth again, most likely to spew another sweet insult, when Xander took her arm.

'Time to go. Don't bother coming back until you can show some civility to my wife.'

'I can walk. You don't need to manhandle me.' She tugged her arm free, finished her drink and handed the empty glass back to him. 'I'll see you in the morning, darling. Don't forget your father's flying to Germany for the Munich Conference so he won't be at the board meeting.' Then she looked at Elizabeth one last time. 'I'll see *you* in court. Goodbye, darlings.'

Only when she was sure Mirela had truly gone, looking through the window as the chauffeured car sped off to make doubly sure, did Elizabeth dare look at Xander.

'My *God*. Your mother is something else.'

He'd poured them both another Scotch and sat himself in one of the rounded pods by the infinity pool, gazing out into the distance with a grim expression on his face.

'I can only apologise.'

'You weren't to know she was coming.'

His head dropped forward and he rubbed the back of his neck. 'For what she said to you.'

'You don't control her mouth.'

'I'm glad you didn't let her intimidate you. I would have cut in sooner but I thought I should see how you handled her.' He lifted his head, his eyes suddenly lightening. 'You handled her beautifully.'

'Better than I would have ten years ago,' she admitted. Ten years ago his mother would have cut her down in flames.

Ironically, it was Xander's dumping of her to supposedly protect her from Mirela that had toughened her up to deal with the witch.

'And don't forget I've had practice with my own mom. I would love to get them in a room together. I have no idea who'd come out as top dog but it would be fun to watch.'

'It sounds like my idea of hell,' he commented drily.

Then the look between them changed, all the amusement dissolving. Her lips began tingling again as she recalled their kiss...

A mistake that wouldn't be repeated.

She crossed her arms tightly across her chest before giving a decisive nod. 'I totally understand why you wouldn't want her to have custody of Loukas. I will do everything in my power to make sure the judge sees us as a loving, stable couple.'

Xander didn't say anything, simply stared at her

in the way that made her veins heat and her belly turn to mush.

The kiss they'd shared loomed like a spectre between them and it was all she could do not to gaze at those firm lips that had covered hers so deliciously.

She edged away to the door with a pounding heart, and cleared her throat. 'What happened before your mother turned up...' She cleared her throat.

He didn't fill the silence.

She shuffled further back. 'It was a mistake.'

His jaw clenched. 'It won't happen again,' he stated flatly, then took another large drink of his Scotch, eyes like steel as they bore into her.

Unable to say another word, she jerked a nod and left.

Her heart was still thumping madly when she reached the safety of her room.

A noise woke her from the light doze she had finally fallen into hours later.

She lifted her head from the pillow but only silence rang out. Just as she'd convinced herself she'd imagined it, she heard it again. A cry.

Throwing the covers off, she jumped out of bed and hurried to unlock her door, then sped down the wide hallway to Loukas's room.

Cautiously, she put her ear to his door at the same moment he cried out again.

Heart pounding, she pushed it open and entered his room.

He was on his bed, his covers kicked off and half on the floor, his little body twisting and turning, whimpers coming from his mouth.

Should she wake him? Or was it only sleepwalkers you weren't supposed to rouse?

Another cry came from him and she quickly placed the covers back on him, then sat beside him and tentatively put a hand on his head.

Maybe she could just soothe him back to a happy dream, she figured, holding her breath as she gently stroked his hair.

It seemed to work. After a while he stopped thrashing and the whimpers lessened until they'd gone entirely.

Her heart almost stopped when his eyes opened.

He stared at her wide-eyed, hardly blinking, his mouth forming a tight miserable line.

Wanting to weep for him, Elizabeth continued to stroke his hair. She didn't speak, hoping he'd be able to see in her eyes that she meant him no harm and only wanted to help.

She remembered so clearly the nightmares she'd suffered as a child, the dreams of finding herself lost and alone. Even as a small child she'd known her parents didn't love her. The one person who had shown her love had been her granny but their time together had been infrequent and fleeting. Elizabeth's mother had despised her mother-in-law and her father had feared her. For Elizabeth her granny had been sent from heaven; a security blanket to love and care for her.

It was in that silent moment that she fully understood why Xander had forced her back into his life. He might be incapable of loving her—or any other woman—but he did love this defenceless little boy. And Loukas loved him. Xander was *his* security blanket in a world where his parents were often incapable of caring for him themselves.

Loukas had learned that adults, Xander excepted, could not be trusted to always be there when he needed them. And, as much as she tried to keep her distance from the little boy, reluctant to form an attachment when she knew her time here was limited and she didn't want him to have to deal with the abandonment of yet another adult—because that was how Loukas would see it; as an abandonment—all she wanted was to wrap her arms tightly around him and smother him in love.

Loukas's eyelids became heavier. She stayed where she was until his rigid frame relaxed, his eyes closed a final time and he turned on his side and burrowed back under his covers.

Placing a gentle kiss on the top of his head, she carefully got back to her feet. Only when she turned to tiptoe out of the room did she see Xander standing in the doorway, wearing nothing but a pair of black boxers.

Xander didn't think his heart had ever felt so full or his chest so tight. For hours he'd lain in his bed, reliving their kiss, castigating himself for starting it, fighting the urge to kick the adjoining door down and get into her bed.

Interspersed with all this had been anger he couldn't rid himself of over his mother's surprise visit.

It shouldn't have been a surprise. His mother was a law unto herself. Both his parents were.

He must have fallen asleep as it had taken him a few moments of disorientation to hear Loukas's cries. Before he could go to him, he'd heard Elizabeth's door open and her soft footsteps treading away. He'd arrived at Loukas's room in time to see her place a hand to his nephew's head.

There had been such tenderness in her touch, such compassion for the child who had shown her nothing but animosity, that all he could do was watch with the most enormous lump in his throat.

Now, as she padded to the door, he stepped back to let her pass and captured the delicate floral scent she carried everywhere.

His blood thickening, he pulled the door to so it was slightly ajar and faced her.

Only soft night lights gave any colour to the hallway, a glow that gave Elizabeth an ethereal quality, highlighting the beauty of her oval face. All she wore was a T-shirt that fell to her knees, which, with her mass of curls springing in every direction, stripped back the years to a time when she'd briefly been the centre point of his world.

It had been her beauty that had first captured his attention but there was nothing unique about beautiful women, especially in his world where imperfections were dealt with in a permanent manner from the minimum legal age, turning all the socialites he'd mixed with into one homogenous face.

Elizabeth's beauty had been matched by her smile, which he'd seen her bestow on everyone she made eye contact with. She'd been kind too, another rarity in his world, opening doors for a chambermaid struggling with an enormous cleaning trolley when it seemed as if no one else had even seen her though she was right there before them. *He* wouldn't have seen her if he hadn't been watching Elizabeth.

She might have matured into a cynical sassy bombshell over the years but the Elizabeth from old was in there too, the warm, generous woman he'd been crazy about, still there, ready to spring out and soothe a defenceless child from a nightmare.

'Thank you,' he said quietly, struggling to speak through the raggedness of his chest.

She sucked her lips in and swallowed. 'He's sleeping now.'

Theos, he ached to touch her again. Her small breasts were like little juts straining through her T-shirt and he so badly wanted to taste them again. He wanted to taste all of her again.

But he'd given his word that it wouldn't happen and he intended to keep it. Unless Elizabeth threw herself at him and demanded he take her, he would keep his hands to himself, no matter how many cold showers he had to take.

* * *

Elizabeth waited for Xander to say something else and break this strange chemical cocktail weaving around them. She couldn't tear her eyes from him.

Her heart hammered and she struggled to breathe. The generous proportions of the hallway shrank around them as she gazed into eyes that swam with unashamed desire and made her lungs close up. A pulse set off low within her, her skin heated…

She wanted him so much. Too much. So much that she was in danger of losing her grip on reality, of turning the clock back to a time when she had believed that love was out there and that the desire she had felt for him *must* translate into love.

These were things she didn't want to feel. Not ever again. She couldn't trust her own heart to do the right thing so she must trust her head and let it keep her grounded in reality.

'We should get some sleep.'

He nodded and put a hand to her cheek, rubbing his thumb gently over her cheekbone.

She closed her eyes, her skin burning under his touch, certain he must be able to see her thundering heart beneath her T-shirt.

There was the lightest brush of lips against hers before she heard a deep inhalation. 'Goodnight, Elizabeth.'

When she opened her eyes, all she could see were the muscles across his back rippling as he walked to his bedroom and shut the door firmly behind him.

* * *

Xander ruffled his nephew's hair. 'Sleep tight. I'll see you in the morning.'

Loukas sat up and hooked his arms around Xander's waist. 'Can I see Mummy again tomorrow?'

'If she's well enough.' He wouldn't make any false promises. Katerina needed a liver transplant. To get this, she would have to be sober for six months. For Katerina to recover and have anything like a normal life, she had to quit drinking. This was an issue in itself as she refused, despite all the evidence including her once glowing complexion now an almost fluorescent yellow, to admit she was an alcoholic. She'd been transferred to a different private hospital, one that was more like a convalescence home. There she was watched twenty-four hours a day and given all manner of counselling. Getting a drink was impossible. For the time being she was safe, even if in denial.

She'd been happy to see Loukas though. Xander had wanted to grab her shoulders and force her to look in her son's face.

If you won't admit your problem and fight to save yourself, do it for him, he'd longed to shout. But shouting wouldn't have changed anything. The change could only come from Katerina herself, a woman who had spent her life controlled by others and who had found her only freedom in the bottom of a bottle of spirits.

He thought of Elizabeth—hell, when *didn't* he think of Elizabeth?

She'd been back in his life for a week. Since their

kiss three nights ago they'd hardly seen anything of each other except during the evening meals they shared with Loukas, during which they were studiously polite to each other.

Elizabeth had taken control of her life in an entirely different way from Katerina. She'd formed her own successful business from nothing after putting herself through college, never giving up even when it meant having to walk miles every day as she didn't have the money to pay a bus fare. He felt intense admiration for that, for driving herself to succeed when it would have been far easier to fail.

Once he'd extricated himself from Loukas's hold, he turned off the bedside light and left the room. It was time for a shower.

Tonight, he and Elizabeth were going to a fundraising gala at the Athens Museum so the three of them and Loukas's nanny were staying the night in Xander's Athens home.

It was the perfect opportunity for them to be photographed together and the gala was for a good cause.

After showering, he shaved, then set about dressing, donning a dark blue suit with a white shirt and striped silver tie. He spent half a minute styling his hair, fastened his cufflinks, dabbed some cologne on, checked his shoes for scuffs and declared himself good to go.

Impulse made him knock on the adjoining door. 'Are you nearly ready?'

'Two minutes. I'll meet you in the living room.'

The two minutes turned into twenty. Just as he

was starting to get annoyed, footsteps sounded down the stairs.

Rising to meet her, he stepped through the living room door and all the air sucked itself from his lungs.

She came to a stop two steps from the bottom of the wide stairs, consternation on her face. 'Well? Am I presentable for Greek society?'

He swallowed to dislodge a boulder jammed in his throat. 'You look…' he shook his head '…ravishing.'

Her full-length couture dress fitted snuggly against her lean body, high-necked with a frill at the cuff of the long sleeves. Dark grey in colour, it was overlaid with a mesh of tiny white metallic roses that glimmered under the light. A thin black belt with a large crystal buckle and a matching purse completed the outfit. She'd swept her mass of hair to one side in a knot at the base of her ear with a crystal fastener, a couple of stray curls left free to soften her oval face. Her eyes were subtly made up while her lips matched the blood red of her fingernails. The whole effect was dramatic and classy and hit him in the groin more effectively than if she'd worn something revealing.

It was only when she took the last remaining steps that he noticed the slit running the entire length of her right leg, right up to mid-thigh, showcasing a pair of sparkling silver heels, and the ache in his groin became altogether harder.

Gritting his teeth, determined not to show his arousal—for God's sake, he was thirty years old, far too old to be getting inappropriate erections—he held out an arm to her.

The slightest of curves tugged on her lips, and she slipped a hand into it.

It was time to face the cameras.

CHAPTER NINE

THE ATHENS MUSEUM was in the Monastiraki neighbourhood, a short distance from Xander's home.

'We could've walked,' Elizabeth said when they came to a stop outside an impressive neoclassical building.

He arched a brow. 'You want to walk in those shoes?'

'Maybe not,' she agreed demurely.

All day she'd had butterflies playing in her belly. Throughout her career she'd acted as a stylist for many of her clients, mostly her female ones. Some were new to a particular section of the wealthy world their date inhabited. Others, unwilling to confide in anyone what they were doing, simply wanted the company. What Elizabeth rarely did was doll herself up and attend a function such as this. When she did it was always with one eye on her watch, looking for the earliest polite time to leave.

Tonight she'd deliberately left her wrist bare and her cell in her room. Like in Diadonus, Xander had put her in the adjoining room to his.

The car door opened and Xander got out. He turned to her and held out a hand.

Meeting his eye, she took it, swinging her legs out in what she hoped was a graceful manner, and was thrown back to a week ago on St Francis when he'd helped her out of the golf buggy at the airport.

It was crazy to think only a week had passed since that evening. She'd gone to bed that night hating him, certain she would never forgive him for his threats and blackmail when a simple explanation of the situation would have been enough to get her agreement.

She felt differently now. Having met Loukas and lived under the same roof as him for almost a week, she understood why Xander had been so determined to bring her here. Having met Mirela, she doubly understood.

It was to protect Loukas from that narcissist woman that she'd determined to be the best wife a man could want. In public in any case. In the privacy of Xander's home it was safer to hide away when he was around.

Tonight though, they were on display to the public and she would play her part to perfection.

It was with this thought in mind that she kept her hand in Xander's, even when she was upright. And it was with this thought in mind that she laced her fingers through his.

The butterflies ratcheted up a notch.

Their evening meal in Diadonus Town had felt like a punishment.

Tonight…

This felt like a date.

She had to remind herself it wasn't a date in the true sense of the term.

And she had to remind herself that she didn't *want* a date with him in any real sense of the word.

But when he let go of her hand and placed his arm around her back to clasp her hip and bring her closer to his side, her frantically beating heart begged to differ.

'You look like you're enjoying yourself,' Xander said when they'd finally been left alone for a few minutes. It seemed every guest there wanted to say hello to the newly-weds who'd actually been married ten years. Their rehearsed story fascinated them. Elizabeth had repeated it so many times she was starting to believe it herself.

'I do? Great. My acting skills are paying off.'

'You're *not* having a good time?'

She considered it, raising her champagne glass to her lips and letting the bubbles play on her tongue. 'I'm not sure. I've been so busy trying to look like I'm having a good time that I haven't had time to wonder if I actually am.'

He laughed. 'You're going to a lot of effort.'

'I don't want your mother hearing that her new old daughter-in-law had a sourpuss look on her face when we're supposed to be showing devotion and happiness.'

'Happiness was never on the list of requirements.'

'It should have been. What couple in love *doesn't* look happy?'

'Look around you,' he said. 'Is there anyone here who looks anything less than happy?'

'That's smugness. It's a different kind of happiness from the happiness that radiates when someone's fool enough to think they're in love.' Ten years ago *she* had radiated in it.

Xander looked so darn gorgeous in that suit. Its colour matched his eyes so well she could believe it had been commissioned specially for it. There was just something about the way he filled a suit and the command in which he wore it... It was incredibly sexy.

He was sexy.

It occurred to her that she should stop drinking.

Silver trays of canapés were brought out. Elizabeth selected a square of pizza with a smile of thanks, and then there was a loud call for silence and they turned to see the museum director climb a podium to begin his talk.

'Are you going to sponsor one of the pieces?' Elizabeth asked, after it had been explained how individuals who donated above a certain—extortionate—amount could select which artefact they wanted their name to appear under when the renovations were complete.

'That's why we're here.'

'Which one do you fancy having your name under?'

He shrugged. 'We're a country with a rich heritage that brings pride to our nation and attracts tourists from all over the world. Preserving that heritage is important and I'm in a position where I can help. It doesn't matter where my name is.'

'Good for you.' From the corner of her eye she spotted a face that made her look twice. Tugging at the sleeve of his suit jacket, she whispered, 'Do you see that couple standing by the chocolate fountain? *Don't* make it obvious.'

Rubbing his head and turning casually, Xander looked. A tiny snicker escaped his throat. 'Little and large?'

'That's the one. I matched them together.'

Morgan Adie was a tech genius from Silicon Valley who barely topped five feet with a stomach almost as wide as his height. His wife, Miranda, was a good foot taller than him with her heels on and rake thin.

'How did you match *them*?'

'Morgan likes tall women with more than one brain cell to rub together. Miranda has a degree in mathematics and likes billionaires. Her only requirement other than money was someone without a hairy back. They've been married for five years now.'

Amusement was evident all over his face. 'Shall we go and say hello?'

'I think they're avoiding us—they're the only guests who haven't introduced themselves.' At his furrowed brow she explained, 'Now the whole world knows what I did for a living, they're worried people will think they know me, put two and two together and come up with four.'

The hours passed, more canapés were eaten,

more champagne drunk. But it didn't drag. Not in the slightest. She hadn't seen Xander so relaxed since he'd forced her back into his life and it felt the most natural thing in the world to mingle with their hands clasped together and the warmth of his body pressed close enough to heat her skin.

Elizabeth had to constantly remind herself that this was all for show, but when they got back in the car at the end of the night, the dividing partition up, blacked-out windows that didn't allow anyone to see in, he made no effort to let go of her hand.

Conversation that had come easily in the museum dried up. The silence was so absolute she could hear his breaths. She could hear the roar of blood pumping through her.

Suddenly she was afraid to move.

She should move her hand from his. But she couldn't. Her hand refused to obey.

The short drive back took for ever, every second feeling like a minute.

When they pulled up outside Xander's four-storey house her heart went into overdrive.

No sex. That's what you both said.

She unlaced her fingers from his. Her hands had clammed up.

The driver opened the door on her side so she got out first. Xander followed and, as they walked up the steps to his front door, placed a hand in the small of her back.

The house was in silence, the only light the soft

glow of a lamp in the reception hall, left on by a member of the staff for them.

Elizabeth removed her shoes and as she straightened she met Xander's gaze and all the oxygen left her body.

The look in his eyes...

She waited breathlessly for him to make his move but he stood quite still, the only movement the pulsing in his eyes.

He was waiting for a signal from her.

He wouldn't make a move without her explicit blessing even if they had to stand there the whole night doing nothing but gazing at each other.

This was her moment to run away and lock herself in her room but her body fought back, the longing careering through her trumping anything like rationality.

But desire had never been based on rationality. And desire didn't have to mean anything unless she chose to make it so and hadn't she decided long ago that love didn't mean anything? And if that was the case then what was she so frightened of?

She wasn't a naïve nineteen-year-old any more. She'd stopped believing in true love when Xander had broken her heart. It was a lesson she should've learned from her parents' experience. She'd been a fool to believe that she would be different.

Some people found love but they were a rarity. For everyone else, lust was the driving force, confused and twisted into believing it was love. When the desire was gone there was nothing left apart from bitter recrimination. Only the lucky ones were left feeling empty.

She would not make that mistake again. Being with Xander again had unleashed a huge box of desire within her but she would not fool herself into believing it was love.

She was older, wiser and had learned how to protect her heart. But that didn't mean she couldn't experience the desire so long as she accepted it for what it was and so long as she accepted it would never go anywhere.

It had been so long…

Her hand trembling, she reached out to touch his face.

His eyes *blazed*…

'Say it,' he commanded.

She exhaled a ragged breath and met his gaze head-on.

'Please, Xander, kiss me.' Her words were barely above a whisper but it was enough. His pupils pulsed and he stepped to her.

Large hands cupped her cheeks, sliding back to loosen the crystal fastener holding her hair in place and letting it fall to the floor while his fingers speared her tumbling hair.

He lowered his head…

Her stomach melted and when his mouth covered hers, heat fired through her veins. Her lips parted and his tongue swept into her mouth; he was kissing her with such passion her knees weakened.

Dear heaven, this was what she needed, what

she craved. Xander, and the all-consuming pleasure he gave.

And everything he gave she returned.

His hands slid down the nape of her neck and she moaned to feel his skin on hers. But not enough. Never enough. Her sensitised flesh wanted to be touched everywhere.

He pulled at her arms and laced his fingers through hers, then raised her hands above her head and pressed them to the wall.

Then he broke the kiss. For a moment he didn't say or do anything, just stared intently at her with eyes that swirled, before saying roughly, 'Not here.'

More than a little dazed, Elizabeth realised they were still in the reception room and that they could be walked in on at any moment.

'Bed?' she whispered.

His chest rose and he kissed her hard. 'Come.'

Feeling as if she were floating, Elizabeth hurried up the stairs holding tightly to his hand. Neither made a sound until he'd shut his bedroom door behind them, thrown his suit jacket and tie onto the floor—she hadn't even noticed him take them off—and pulled her back into his arms with a groan.

'*Theos*, Elizabeth. You're driving me mad.'

'In a good or bad way?'

'Both.' And then he twisted her round so her back was to him. He gathered all her hair together and lifted it high and pressed a kiss beneath her ear.

She shivered with pleasure. Little moans flew from her throat as he undid the top button of her dress and found the hidden zipper. He pulled it down all the way to her bottom, trailing his tongue down her spine to follow before kissing back up to her neck.

Exquisite sensation flooded her, her body responding to his caresses with unbound delight.

His breath hot in her hair, he took each arm in turn and gently manipulated them out of the sleeves while she unbuckled the skinny belt around her waist. Nipping at her ear, he took hold of the material at her waist and tugged her dress past her hips and let it fall to the floor.

Now all she had on were her bra and panties. Even that felt like too much.

Xander pressed himself flush against her. His arousal was thick through the fabric of his clothes, his erection pushing into the small of her back. His hands bit into her flesh and swept up her thighs and over her belly, cupping her aching breasts for the briefest of moments then sweeping up to her shoulders and bunching her hair together again.

He stilled for a moment and she closed her eyes. Her senses were in overload, the need to touch and taste him...

She twisted round to face him and slid her arms over his shoulders, finding his mouth to devour it with kisses.

He held her tightly, muttering incomprehensible words into her mouth while she worked frantically, pulling at his shirt to loosen it from his trousers. Fumbling with his buttons until she could yank it apart, with a breath of relief she pressed herself against him, chest against chest, skin against skin, the lace of her bra the only barrier between their top halves. She could feel his heart beating and grabbed at his head, catching her breath as she stared into the dark blue eyes that contained as much desire in them as she knew echoed from hers.

It had always been like this; one kiss enough to ignite the fire that burned for him and only him. And now she didn't want to fight it. She wanted to exalt in it. She wanted to let it burn.

He felt so solid in her arms, his skin smoother than she remembered. But his kisses were every bit as greedy as they'd been before, plundering her mouth as she plundered his in turn.

Heaven had come into her life ten years ago in the form of Xander Trakas and now, for one night, she would experience it again and she would revel in every minute of it. How could she fight something that grew so strongly within her, a physical connection she had never found or wanted with anyone else?

But she didn't want to think. All she wanted was to feel. And in Xander's arms, pleasure was the only feeling to be had.

Impatient sensations hurtled through her skin from her head to her toes, every part straining closer to him, desperate to lose the last barrier between them.

Xander must have felt it too for he released his hold on her to put his hands at the belt of his trousers as hers went to her bra and panties. His lips brushed reverently across her cheeks and nuzzled into her neck, then he unbuckled his belt and tugged his pants and boxers off, freeing himself.

A breathless sigh escaped her mouth as their lips found each other again and now, when they came together, every part of her that could touched him. His erection pressed right above her pubis, teasingly out of reach to where she really wanted it to be, and she ground against him, silently pleading.

And then she was swept up in his arms and he carried her to his bed.

Flat on her back, Elizabeth reached out her arms for him but he gave the smallest of smiles and sat beside her. His eyes glistening, his chest rising and falling in a tight rhythm, he placed his fingers on her belly and gently traced a circle around her navel.

Shivers raced down her spine and spread out, and she closed her eyes as he slowly traced his hands over her, stroking her breasts before dipping his head to take one in his mouth.

Sharp, acute pleasure speared her. The heat within her liquefied and she gasped. Then he moved his attention to her other aching breast, his wandering hands making circular motions over her shoulders and then down to her belly.

His lips moved from her breasts and up her neck, fire spreading through her flesh. He reached her mouth and nipped her bottom lip.

'You're even more beautiful than I remember,' he murmured into her mouth, his breath merging with hers. His eyes held hers with an intensity that made the need inside her deepen, and he lowered his hand down onto her pubis and then lower still.

He slid a finger into her heat. She gasped again and clasped her thighs together to hold him there, in the place she most ached.

His eyes swirled, a thousand desires gleaming from that one look, and then his mouth was on hers and he was moving on top of her.

When he covered her completely, he kissed her again, a lingering yet gentle brush of the lips that filled her heart in the same way he filled the rest of her.

With one hand burrowed in her hair, he ran the other down her stomach and to her thigh, gently parting it before nudging the other aside too.

His erection was now pressed against the top of her thigh. It was so close to where she wanted it to be yet so far away. She grabbed his buttocks, kneading her fingers into the tight flesh, and writhed beneath him, urging him on.

He groaned and half pulled away. 'We need protection.'

Elizabeth's head reeled. If he hadn't mentioned it, protection would never have crossed her mind.

What was *happening* to her?

He yanked his bedside drawer open and groped in it, removing a silver square, which he ripped open. He made deft work of putting it on, then his mouth found hers again and he shifted enough for his erection to be right there, where she needed. Raising her thighs a touch, she pushed forward at the same moment he thrust inside her.

Her last conscious thoughts evaporated.

The feel of him inside her…

It felt like heaven.

She didn't think she had ever wanted him so much, not even in their heady lust-driven weeks of old. This was something else, the pleasure so intense that all she wanted was to hold on to it for ever.

Bound as tightly as two lovers could be, they moved in a slow, sensuous rhythm, lips locked together, the only sounds muffled gasps and tiny moans.

Not even heaven could feel this good.

His groin meshed against her pubis, intensifying the sensations happening inside her. One hand clasping his buttock to drive him in ever deeper, her other hand raced up and down the back she had never imagined she would scratch again and she embraced the growing pulsations within her until she was driven over the edge and into the blissful land of heightened pleasure that overcame her senses and drowned out everything else, locking her to him completely.

Xander's groans deepened. His movements gained in fever, carrying her climax with him until he shuddered in her arms and thrust one long last time, so tightly inside her she felt every moment of it, and then he slumped down, his face buried in the crook of her neck.

His strong heartbeat echoed through her skin to

her own skittering heart, and she drifted a lazy hand across his back, marvelling at the strength she found there, awed at the strength of her climax, at her feelings…everything.

'I must be squashing you,' he murmured into her neck a short while later.

'Only a little bit.' Quite a bit in truth but at that moment she felt so blissed out she didn't care. She wasn't yet ready to break the bond.

His muffled laugh played across her skin. He raised his head and kissed her before climbing off and heading to his bathroom.

Elizabeth sighed and closed her eyes.

The euphoria of their lovemaking was already seeping away, memories of the black days after he'd ended it between them, when she would wake praying it had all been a bad dream, flooding her in its wake.

Those were days she would never go back to. Her feelings for him were already dangerous and she couldn't afford to let them deepen further. Spending the night entangled in his arms was a danger too far.

By the time Xander returned, she'd gathered her clothes together.

He came to an abrupt halt to see her standing there.

Affecting nonchalance, she attempted a breezy smile. 'I need to go back to my room. Loukas will be upset if he finds me in here.'

Xander, still trying to get a handle on what had just occurred between them, stared at her and tried to dissect what was going on in her head. When they'd been making love her eyes had been full of passion. Now the familiar shutters had come back down.

What they'd just shared had been better than anything he could have imagined. Better than he remembered it being and it had been damned spectacular then.

He'd felt as if he were a part of her.

And now she stood at the adjoining door acting as cool as if what they'd shared had been nothing but a pleasant interlude in a busy day.

And then he saw it. A flash of vulnerability.

For a spark of time he saw the old Elizabeth.

Yes. She should leave. Right now.

He ran a hand through his hair and gave a curt nod.

She hesitated only a moment, then gave a tight, awkward nod and slipped through the adjoining door.

She disappeared so quickly he could almost believe he'd imagined everything that had just happened.

CHAPTER TEN

XANDER ROLLED OVER, looked at his watch and gave a start. It was ten a.m.

He hadn't slept in so late for years.

All those nights of patchy sleep had finally caught up with him.

Taking a quick shower, he dried, brushed his teeth and threw on a pair of jeans and an old T-shirt.

He found Elizabeth in the dining room sipping from a mug of coffee and reading something on her cell. Opposite her, drinking a glass of milk and playing on his tablet, was Loukas.

They both looked up when he entered the room. Loukas's smile was wide, displaying his mouth of gappy teeth. Elizabeth's smile was polite but wary.

His chest tightened to see her and he was immediately assailed with images of their lovemaking.

She'd clearly been up for hours, her drying curls springing in whatever direction they fancied. All he could see of what she wore was a long-sleeved black top. He wondered if she had anything on her feet and if she'd kept the blood-red varnish on her toenails.

With great effort, he slid onto the chair beside Loukas. 'Have you two had breakfast?'

Loukas nodded, then said in Greek, 'I wanted to come and see you but she said I wasn't to wake you.'

He didn't look at Elizabeth when he said *she* but for once Xander didn't detect any animosity. If anything, the atmosphere between them when he'd walked in had been, if not comfortable, not *un*comfortable.

'Speak in English,' Xander chided gently before asking where Loukas's nanny, Rachael, was.

'She's popped out for an hour,' Elizabeth said, not looking up from her screen. 'I said I'd sit with Loukas.'

'Are we going to see Mummy?' Loukas asked.

'I'll give the clinic a ring and see how she is.'

'Can you call them now?'

'Okay.'

Xander made the call, his gaze drifting to Elizabeth as he spoke to the duty manager.

Theos, he could look at her for hours and never tire of the view.

He pushed thoughts of her naked breasts from his mind and put his attention to the call in hand.

'We can visit,' he confirmed when he'd finished.

Loukas beamed and excused himself. Xander knew his nephew was going to his room to select an outfit that would please Katerina. He'd done the same thing with his own mother when he'd been Loukas's age. Starved for her company, he would make a huge effort when he knew he would be seeing her, always hopeful of an approving smile if not physical affection. A pat on the head was the most he or Yanis could have hoped for.

By the time Xander hit adolescence, he'd stopped hoping for any parent-son interaction and learned that to get attention from them all he needed to do was show interest in the family business.

As far as his parents were concerned, it went without saying that their sons would join the company. It was what generations of Trakases had done, future spouses selected on what they could bring to it. Mirela, Xander's mother, had been the heiress of a luxury cosmetics company that had been gobbled up to sit alongside the rest of the Timos SE lines.

Unlike other Trakas spouses, Mirela had never been content to sit at home and play the dutiful wife and mother. An only child, she had been taught by her father everything there was to know about the cosmetics industry and she'd married Dragan Trakas with a determination to be an asset in the boardroom rather than the bedroom. Xander would admire her refusal to be pigeonholed as a wealthy adornment if she hadn't been so inherently selfish.

Dragan and Mirela had formed a powerful union and taken Timos from strength to strength while severely neglecting their sons in the process. Until, that was, their sons were old enough to be taught the mechanisms of business.

Yanis had gone along with it half-heartedly. Business didn't interest him. He'd wanted to be a musician but that had never been an option for him.

Xander had grabbed the opportunity with both hands. He'd been determined to outshine both his parents. He'd soaked up every crumb of information they threw at him, spent hours going through the accounts of the varying divisions, learnt the name of every employee in their Athens head office then progressed to the names of those in their European branches. If they'd had an American division he would have learnt those employee names too, but the US had proved to be a market his parents were unable to crack. Critics said their products were *'too European'*, whatever that meant.

When he'd returned from St Francis it had been with a renewed determination to not only live his life under his own terms but to be master of his own destiny and in the process wreak revenge on his parents for their part in Ana's death and the steady ruin of Yanis's life.

He'd made a deal with them. He would launch their products in North America and turn a hundred-million-dollar operating profit within three years. If he succeeded, they were to step down as joint bosses and pass the mantle to him. They'd been so dismissive of him succeeding where they had failed that they'd agreed. Indeed, they'd laughed at him. If *they* couldn't succeed in the American market then he certainly couldn't.

They hadn't reckoned on his stubbornness or the anger that fuelled him. He had no doubt he could make a success of himself elsewhere but that wouldn't give the same satisfaction as wresting control of his parents' own company and shifting the balance of power into his own hands.

Three years to the day after they'd made their deal, Xander became the official boss of Timos SE. His parents' had never forgiven him, even though he'd kept them on, valuing their business acumen and talents. In that one regard he was like his parents— why cut off an asset that was making you money?

Now, alone with Elizabeth, who was still studying her phone, he was awash with memories of how he'd constantly needed to touch her all those years ago. He hadn't been able to keep his hands off her, and not just because he'd wanted to be inside her all the time. She'd been the same with him. They couldn't even eat a simple meal without locking their ankles together. It was a relationship like nothing he'd experienced before, as intense as the descent of the steepest roller coaster.

If there wasn't a steady flow of staff busy around the villa he would be tempted to take her in his arms right then.

'Would you like to visit Katerina with us?'

She put her phone down. 'I don't think that's a good idea.'

'She's curious to meet you.'

'Loukas is just starting to get used to me. I don't want to ruin it by barging in on his time with his mother. He won't see her for another week and doesn't need me intruding on their time together.'

He gazed at her through narrowed eyes. 'Or is it that you don't want to spend time with him?'

He'd seen the affection she had for Loukas the other night during his nephew's nightmare but it concerned him that she seemed unwilling to draw him out of the shell he formed when she was around.

To her credit she didn't pretend not to understand what he was talking about. She sighed and scrunched her hair in her hands. 'I don't want to push him, Xander. He's a scared little boy and any friendship has to come from him. I do want him to be comfortable with me—that's why I was happy to amuse myself on my phone while he played with his tablet, so he could just *be* while with me, but I'm wary of getting too close. If he gets too used to me it'll be even harder on him when I go back to New York.'

Needles dragged up his spine at the mention of her going back.

He rubbed his forehead with a knuckle and gave a stiff nod.

A member of his household staff came into the dining room with his breakfast and a fresh pot of coffee.

Elizabeth watched Xander cut into his poached egg on toast and her heart beat a little faster. There was something about the way his throat moved when he ate that made her belly tighten and her heart want to weep.

She cradled her coffee with both hands and gazed at the priceless paintings that lined the walls of this great room. Xander's Athens home was as grand as his Diadonus one but had a darker, more oppressive feel to it.

She longed to return to Diadonus and the lightness she found there.

She could feel his gaze on her, and closed her eyes as fresh memories of Xander being deep inside her rushed through her, turning her insides into liquid…

'How do you understand Loukas so well?'

Her head was so filled with their lovemaking that it took a moment to understand what he was asking.

'I was like him at that age,' she said simply when she'd gathered her thoughts together. 'Lost.'

'Is that when your parents divorced?'

'It's when they decided their marriage was over. Loukas's mom's and dad's addictions are very public so he'll be dealing with school friends asking questions about it and telling him the "facts" they've picked up when listening to their own parents discuss it.'

His brows drew together. 'You've dealt with something similar?'

'My parents' divorce got so vicious it made the New York dailies.'

He gave a slow shake of his head.

'They spent so much on legal fees fighting each other over the silliest things that the judge basically hauled them into court and gave them a public dressing down.' She gathered all her hair together in a big bunch at the nape of her neck and sighed. 'They're both attorneys so you'd think they'd know better.'

'What started it all? Did one of them have an affair?'

'The one thing they both agree on is that there was

nothing specific. It was an accumulation of things. I can't remember a time when they weren't at loggerheads. I was seven when Dad filed for divorce but they lived under the same roof for five more years because neither of them was prepared to give any ground. They both wanted the house and all the contents. They were like a pair of big cats marking their territory in it.'

'Who got the house?'

'Neither of them. They were ordered to sell it and split the proceeds.' She dropped her hold on her hair and swallowed back the nausea thinking of this period always induced. 'I was so relieved when they finally got their own homes. I honestly thought things would get better if they weren't in each other's faces every day but, jeez, it got worse. Both of them were determined to believe the other had diddled them and sneaked out stuff belonging to the other. Can you believe my mom reported my dad to the police over a photo frame?'

Xander's breathing had become heavy. When she dared look at him she saw his features had darkened.

'Who got custody of you?' he asked tightly.

'They had to share me, which pleased neither of them. One week with Mom, the next with Dad. No deviations apart from Thanksgiving and Christmas, which I was court-mandated to alternate between them. They both fought it. Dad became vegetarian just to spite her and tried to get a court order to force her to only feed me vegetarian food too. Mom retaliated by trying to pay a doctor to falsely diagnose me

with anaemia, which she could blame on the vege-
tarianism and so declare him a bad father.'

She'd been like a toy to be played with. A weapon
to be used against the other. They hadn't loved her.
They just hadn't wanted the other to have her.

Xander's stomach churned violently, cold fury
sweeping through him at such despicable behaviour from the people who'd been supposed to love
and protect her. 'Some people don't deserve to have
children.'

'Agreed,' she replied softly, looking away from
him and blinking rapidly. 'They only married because she got pregnant. They were united in their
belief the other was at fault for that too.'

A sudden burst of mirthless laughter escaped
from her. 'If I were to write a book about them everyone would think it was fiction. No one would believe
two fully grown people could behave so childishly.'

Xander couldn't even bring himself to smile. His
fury remained, coiling like a snake in his chest.

There were many words to describe her parents'
behaviour. Childish was the mildest of them, by far.

He thought of how Elizabeth had been all those
years ago: open-hearted, warm and optimistic. He'd
taken her at face value, never dreaming that she'd
lived through such hell.

How could someone so loving come from a union
mired in such bitterness?

Their conversation was interrupted when Loukas's nanny came in, back from her short trip out
and looking for her charge.

Elizabeth jumped to her feet, thankful for the interruption. Remembering those horrible years was never easy but worse was remembering how desperately she'd clung to the belief that her life would be different. She would marry the right person for her and it would be true love that lasted for ever. The children they had would be so loved they would never doubt their own worth for a second.

She must—*must*—remember her old romantic ideals were nothing but a myth.

A myth she'd contributed to, she acknowledged ruefully. She'd gone to St Francis full of romantic dreams but also, she now realised, grieving for her grandmother. Her granny had been the only person in the world to love her, and, though their time together had been limited, Elizabeth had adored everything about her. Her death had devastated her.

When she'd arrived in St Francis she'd been that deadly combination of vulnerable and idealistic. She'd been desperate for love, and so willing to throw caution to the wind when love finally presented itself in the form of Xander.

'I've got some stuff I need to catch up on,' she said, already heading for the door.

'I thought you'd wrapped the business up.'

'I've a few loose ends to sort.'

He nodded. 'I'll take Loukas to visit Katerina and then we can get something to eat before we return to Diadonus.'

She smiled her agreement and left, thankful to make her escape without discussing the one thing that had echoed between them. The night they'd spent together.

She knew that when they next found themselves alone again, things would be different.

While Xander took Loukas to visit Katerina, Elizabeth took a cab to Monastiraki, wanting to explore the area that had captured her attention through the car's window the previous evening. As it was Sunday, most shops were closed, but there was a flea market to wander around before she found a small art museum to while away more time. None of the art particularly grabbed her attention but it had an excellent gift shop and she spent an age browsing the goods.

She trailed her fingers over the notebooks, remembering her obsession with stationery when she'd been young. When she'd moved out of her mother's house, she'd binned almost one hundred notebooks filled with childish scribblings, a childhood where she'd created her own worlds on paper, worlds where parents loved their children and there was someone for everyone to love.

She hadn't written anything creative in ten years. The notebooks she'd used for her business had always been plain and professional-looking.

On impulse, she snatched a notebook up. Its cover was a reprint of a gorgeous nude painting of a woman sleeping. Helping herself to another and a couple of pretty pens, she paid for her purchases with a thumping heart.

For the first time in a decade she felt the compulsion to write. To create.

Back out in the cool sun, she fished for her shades and found a café to wait for Xander at, firing off a message to him with her location.

While she waited, she sipped on a coffee and, a slight tremor in her hands, removed one of the notebooks' clear wrappings.

Xander's driver dropped them off round the corner from the café Elizabeth was waiting at for him.

Holding Loukas's hand, he passed through the throngs of people meandering through the streets.

He spotted her immediately, alone at a table, shades atop her curly hair, her head bent forward. As they got closer, he saw she was writing. It was a sight that inexplicably made his heart clench.

'You look busy,' he said when they reached her.

She dropped the pen and looked up, colour suffusing her cheeks as she sat her forearm over her notebook.

He liked that she blushed to see him. He very much liked that her eyes took on a glazed look when he held them with his.

He could hardly wait to get her alone.

'Just passing the time.' She shoved the book in her bag, then pulled out a different notebook with a reprint of a painting depicting Zeus on its cover and handed it, along with a pen, to Loukas. 'A present for you,' she said with a smile.

After a moment's hesitation, Loukas took them and studied the notebook carefully.

'Thank you,' he whispered in English.

Startled amber eyes met his. As far as Xander was aware, they were the first words his nephew had spoken to Elizabeth since he'd told her to go away.

His chest swelled but he took pains not to show it. 'Shall we eat here?'

Loukas took a seat. It was as far from Elizabeth as he could get but at least he didn't curl his body away from her.

As Elizabeth studied her menu, and Loukas unwrapped his notebook, Xander studied Elizabeth and was consumed with the urge to unwrap *her*.

'Have a drink with me,' Xander said, pouring himself a Scotch.

Loukas's nanny had just whisked him away from the dining table for a bath and Elizabeth had stood too, looking ready to bolt.

She hesitated.

'I'm requesting a drink, not to rip your clothes off. Unless,' he added when her eyes found his, 'you want me to rip them off.'

'Look, Xander…' She perched her bottom on the edge of the table and dragged her teeth over her bottom lip. 'Last night was great.'

'It was,' he agreed. A twinge pulled at his groin as he recalled for the hundredth time that day just how great it had been.

Pouring a liberal dose of gin in a glass for her, he

added two cubes of ice, a slice of lemon, and topped it up with tonic water.

He took it over and held it out to her.

'I didn't say I wanted one,' she said softly, accepting it nonetheless.

He deliberately brushed his fingers against hers. 'You didn't say no.'

A curl had fallen onto her face. He pushed it away then dove his hand into her thick mass of hair.

Her breath hitched. 'Xander...'

'I've been fantasising about you all day.' He pressed his cheek against hers so his words flowed into her ear. Her beautiful scent played into his senses, heating him. 'Have you been thinking of me?'

'I've been with you for most of the day,' she protested, but made no attempt to escape his hold or move her soft cheek from his.

He moved his mouth over hers and nipped her bottom lip. 'All I've wanted today is to get you alone.'

He took the glass from her hand and set it on the table, then used his thighs to nudge her legs apart so he stood between them. Her eyes gleamed and he knew she could feel his arousal through the thick denim of the jeans they both wore.

'You're here. I'm here,' he murmured, brushing his lips across her skin as he spoke. 'We both want each other. We both know how good the sex is between us. The genie's out of the bottle and it's not going back in.'

He trailed his fingers down her spine, delighting in the little shivers she gave at his touch. He kissed her then looked deep into her bright eyes. 'We both know where we stand. No false hopes. No one gets hurt.'

She gazed at him for an almost insufferable length of time before she sighed and wound her arms around his neck.

'No one gets hurt,' she agreed with a whisper. Then her lips parted and she was kissing him, her hold around his neck tightening as she pressed her chest to his.

The ache in his groin worse than ever, Xander devoured her mouth, plundering it as he leaned her back so she was almost flat on the table.

How badly he wanted to be inside her.

A discreet cough shattered the moment.

Loukas's nanny stood in the doorway, bright red with embarrassment. 'Loukas left his new notebook in here.'

Xander pulled away from a clearly mortified Elizabeth. The notebook was on the table next to her delectable bottom.

Once Rachael had disappeared he took a drink of his Scotch. Elizabeth was still cringing from her perch on the table.

'Sometimes I think I employ too many staff,' he said drily, adjusting his jeans, which had become painfully constricting.

Given the opportunity he would lock her in a secluded retreat, just the two of them, and make love to her until they were both so sated neither could walk.

She took a sip of her gin with a trembling hand

but her voice was steady and her gaze unwavering as she said, 'And I think an early night is called for.'

He raised his glass in a salute and adjusted his jeans again with a wince. 'I'll drink to that.'

Five hours later, Xander watched Elizabeth collect her strewn clothing from the mess on floor. By the time they'd got to his bedroom they'd been so desperate for each other they hadn't even made it into the bed. He'd taken her against the door with only a fraction of their clothing removed.

Afterwards, they'd taken a shower together then got into bed and taken each other all over again.

She noticed him watching her and smiled. 'Next time you can do the walk of shame.'

'Through an adjoining door?'

She laughed softly and blew him a kiss.

Resisting the urge to ask her to stay, he said only, 'You know where my bed is if you want another repeat.'

'Goodnight, Xander.'

The last sound he heard from her room was the adjoining door being locked.

CHAPTER ELEVEN

Now they were officially lovers again, the antipathy Elizabeth had been holding on to seeped from her like a slowly deflating balloon.

Their lives over the next few days took on a routine. Xander would fly to Athens early each morning after they'd breakfasted with Loukas, while she would take a long walk along the beach. Once back in his villa, she would set herself up in the infinity room with her notebook. Within a couple of days she'd filled it. When she asked Xander if she could hitch a lift with him to Athens he readily agreed, suggesting they meet for an early lunch.

Alone there, she found an excellent stationery shop, made her purchases, then decided to take a wander around the vibrant city. As she passed a news stand, the front cover of a paper caught her eye. It had a photo of her and Xander on it, taken at the museum fundraiser four days ago.

It was a vivid reminder of why she was there.

The court case was only two days away.

Studying the picture some more, she could see

it had been taken when they'd first arrived at the museum, mere hours before they'd become lovers again, when she'd still been determined to fight her attraction to him.

The nights they shared were wonderful but, no matter how deeply sated she was or how badly she longed to sleep in his arms, she wouldn't spend the night with him. It was safer that way.

As wary as she was of Loukas forming an attachment to her, she was doubly wary of allowing herself to form an attachment to Xander.

She would not leave herself open to heartbreak again. It had been hard enough to get over him the first time.

But you never really got over him, did you? If you had you wouldn't have spent the rest of your life alone.

It was a thought she kept shoving away, scared to even dwell on it.

She found the restaurant she'd agreed to meet Xander at and, the sun shining down, decided to take an outside table. While she waited, her cell rang.

She pressed the accept button at the moment she spotted Xander heading towards her and raised her hand in greeting.

When he reached her, she rose to kiss him then carried on with her conversation.

'Who was that?' he asked when she'd finished the call.

'Steve.'

Was she imagining it or did Xander's jaw clench?

'I thought you'd got everything wrapped up about Leviathan Solutions?'

No, she wasn't imagining it. There was a definite edge to his voice.

'He was calling to catch up.'

'Catch up? Friends catch up.'

'And Steve's a friend. He wanted to tell me about the temp work he's found and how awful his new colleagues are.'

His fingers drummed on the table. 'Are you lovers?'

She reared back a little. 'Are you insane? How many times do I have to tell you we're just friends?'

'You never answered the question properly before. Friends are capable of being lovers. It happens all the time.'

Her cheeks now scarlet, Elizabeth leaned over the table and said, 'What does it matter? I don't drill you on your sex life.'

'That's it though. I don't know anything about who you've been involved with.' Xander dragged a hand through his hair. 'You know everything about my past relationships—including the ones that never happened,' he added with a grin that belied the undercurrents racing through his veins. Whenever he heard the name Steve he wanted to thump something.

That she'd been his wife all these years was neither of their faults and he accepted he had no right to feel possessive towards her. It didn't change the fact that he *did* feel possessive.

It was a level of possessiveness he hadn't felt for many years. Ten of them.

'That's your own fault.' She showed no sign of softening.

'Those stories about me were bull and you know it. I was barely on first-name terms with half the women who said they'd shared my bed.'

Her eyes flashed. 'Bull or not, it doesn't give you the right to know every aspect of my life and your petty jealousy isn't going to make me tell you anything.'

'I'm not jealous.'

'Then don't act like you are.'

Xander had never been jealous in his life. The idea was ridiculous.

And yet…

The thought of another man touching her made him want to do more than thump things.

He rolled his neck and forced a deep breath. 'Let's change the subject to something neutral.'

After all, with Loukas's custody case only two days away, the last thing they needed was to have a public argument. The restaurant was busy and, judging by the side-eye they were getting from most of the other diners and passers-by, they'd been recognised.

'Can you ask your pilot to take me home?' Elizabeth asked when she'd had enough. 'I don't want to hang around here for the rest of the day.'

Now that she had her new notebooks, she was

itching to get back to the script idea slowly unfolding in her head.

Also, watching Xander spear his chicken pieces as if they'd personally offended him had affected her appetite. If they'd been in the privacy of his home she would have had it out with him but being in public she'd held her tongue and contented herself with throwing daggers at him with her eyes.

Was he really jealous of Steve? And if he was, what did that mean? That he was developing feelings for her?

He raised a shoulder and pulled his phone out. 'Sure.'

He made the call and then looked at her. His lips, which had been pressed in a thin line, softened. 'Do I get a kiss goodbye?'

'Are you going to say sorry for being a butthead?'

'A what…?' His eyes narrowed but then he grinned and shook his head. 'I'm sorry for being a butthead.'

'Apology accepted.'

'Now do I get a kiss goodbye?'

'For the sake of the cameras?' There were no lurking photographers that she could see.

His eyes gleamed. 'Why else?'

Xander had arranged for a cab to meet her at the Diadonus airstrip. When Elizabeth walked into the villa she understood why he hadn't got a member of staff to collect her. It was market day in Diadonus Town and all the staff had gone there.

Wandering into the kitchen to make herself a coffee, she was searching for cups when her cell rang.

'Are you home?' Xander asked without preamble.

'I've just walked in. What's up?'

'I've had a call from the school. Loukas has fallen out of a tree—he's okay but they think he might have fractured his arm. I'm on my way to the airport but it's going to be a good hour until I get there. It's Rachael's day off so I need you to collect him for me and take him to the medical centre.'

'Me?'

'The school's expecting you. Take one of my cars. The keys are in the top drawer of my desk in my study. I'll meet you at the medical centre.'

Before she could protest that she hadn't driven a car in over a decade, the line went dead.

Oh, well, she'd explain about her lack of driving experience when she got into an accident or something.

Oh, God, she had to drive Loukas in it too. As if the poor kid hadn't suffered enough.

Mentally trying to remember the mechanics of driving, she sped to Xander's study and found his collection of keys where he'd said they would be and took the first set that came to hand.

Entering the enormous garage, which was more like a hangar and filled with dozens of the world's most famous and expensive cars in a neat row, she clicked the key until she spotted a car's lights flashing.

It was the black Porsche Spyder.

She hit the button to open the main garage doors then scratched her head trying to figure how to get into the car. Once she'd managed that she stared at the spectacular array of gizmos and gadgets feeling rather dizzy and wondering how on earth she started the thing.

She'd learned to drive when she was sixteen but had never owned a car and hadn't got behind the wheel since she quit Brown. She much preferred walking and, besides, New York was a nightmare for traffic.

She put the Porsche into gear and, sending a prayer to the God of Not Pranging Xander's Car, inched forward and stalled it. After many starts, stalls and splutters she finally drove out of the garage and onto the open road.

Terrified of what she would find at the school, she parked badly at the front of the building and hurried into the reception.

The headmistress was waiting for her and looked at her with much suspicion. In her hand was a newspaper. It took Elizabeth a moment to realise it was the paper she'd seen in Athens earlier with her and Xander on the front. The head was satisfying herself Elizabeth really was Xander's wife and therefore a person she could admit into her school.

'He fell from tree,' the headmistress said. 'He was hiding.'

'Is it only his arm that's hurt?'

'*Nai.*'

'Where else is he injured?' she asked in alarm before remembering *nai* was the Greek word for yes.

She was taken to a small room where a white-faced Loukas sat on a sofa, a young serious-faced woman beside him. Someone had made a sling for his damaged arm.

When he saw her his little face crumpled.

Kneeling before him, Elizabeth said gently, 'How are you feeling?'

Loukas didn't answer but tears started to fall.

'Your arm hurts?'

He nodded.

'Your uncle's on his way home. He's asked me to take you to the medical centre to get it looked at.'

Now he shook his head violently.

'The doctor will be able to give you medicine to make you feel better,' she cajoled.

More head shaking.

'Don't you want your arm to be better?'

A slight hesitation then a nod.

'So why don't you want to come with me? Your uncle will meet us there.'

So used to her every question being met with muteness, Elizabeth thought she was hearing things when his lips parted and he whispered something.

'What did you say, honey?'

She leaned closer and tucked her hair behind her ear so he could speak into it, half expecting him to say he'd rather suffer his broken arm than go anywhere with her.

'The doctor will keep me there.'

'No…' As she immediately repudiated his words,

she thought of his mother and understood where his fears were coming from.

His mother had gone to hospital a month ago and there was no sign of her coming home any time soon.

'Loukas,' she tried again, 'I promise you, they won't keep you there. If your arm is broken they might have to keep you in overnight—I'm not a doctor so I don't know, but I promise, cross my heart, that you will come home very soon.'

'I don't want to be on my own.'

She could cry for him.

'Your uncle won't let that happen and neither will I. One of us will stay with you the whole time.'

'You promise?'

She made a solemn sign of the cross over her chest. 'I promise.'

Loukas seemed to think about it before giving a tentative nod.

Elizabeth held out a hand to him. 'Shall we get your arm fixed now?'

The arm that wasn't in a sling reached out. A little hand slipped into hers.

That one simple, trusting gesture melted her heart completely.

Xander made the journey to the medical centre ready to ram cars and people for not moving fast enough.

When he finally pulled up in the car park, he spotted his Porsche Spyder, sticking out like a sore thumb parked as it was almost diagonally over two spaces.

Despite the worry gnawing at him it was a sight that brought a wry smile to his face.

He knew he'd been unfair passing the responsibility for Loukas onto Elizabeth's shoulders but he hadn't been able to think of another option. It wasn't that he thought her incapable of caring for his nephew; quite the opposite, but he was worried about Loukas's reaction to her. His nephew seemed no closer to accepting her as a presence in his life and Xander had to keep reminding himself that Elizabeth was doing the right thing in not forcing it seeing as she wasn't going to be a part of it for ever.

The medical centre had opened in Diadonus only four years ago and was like a miniature hospital with first-class medical staff, state-of-the-art scanners and even an operating theatre.

The lady working behind the reception desk recognised him and sent him off with a smile to the paediatric ward. There, he found them in a private room. They were both sitting on the bed, Elizabeth reading him a story.

They both smiled widely to see him.

To Xander's amazement, Loukas was holding her hand.

Elizabeth saw the direction of his gaze and gave him a look that clearly said, 'Do not say *anything*.'

Pulling up a chair to sit beside them, Xander made the usual small talk such circumstances necessitated, doing his best to be nonchalant about Loukas's arm and the fact he seemed to have finally accepted Elizabeth.

He never had a chance to dissect it as the doctor came into the room.

'I have good and bad news,' he said in Greek, addressing Xander. 'The arm is broken but it's a clean fracture.'

'Will I need an operation?' Loukas asked.

'Yes, young man.'

'But I want to go home.'

'If we get the operation done today there's no reason you can't go home tomorrow.'

Elizabeth was watching this exchange intently, a puzzled look on her face.

'The doctor says I need an operation,' Loukas told her forlornly in English.

'Cool! You'll get your arm put in plaster and everyone will draw silly pictures on it.'

To Xander's complete amazement—as if the past ten minutes hadn't provided enough of it—Loukas cheered up.

The doctor raised his clipboard. 'The anaesthetist's on her way. The rest of the team's ready. We'll do the operation in around an hour, so shall we get the paperwork signed?'

Sitting in the family room while Loukas was being operated on was tantamount to torture. All Xander could see was his nephew's brave little face as the mask that would put him to sleep was placed over him.

He knew it was only a routine operation but Loukas had looked so vulnerable and pale on that theatre bed.

He'd wanted both Xander and Elizabeth there and had made them both promise to be there when he woke up.

It had been Elizabeth's breeziness about the whole thing that, he was certain, had stopped Loukas's nerves. Judging by her wan complexion now, it had all been an act put on to stop a little boy's fears. She was just as worried as he was.

'Did Loukas tell you what happened?' he asked quietly.

'He was hiding.'

'Who? Loukas?'

'Yes. His classmates were all playing tag. He didn't want to play so he hid in the tree.'

'Why didn't he just say he didn't want to play?'

'He thought they would laugh at him.'

'He told you this?'

She nodded.

A nurse came in with another coffee for them.

'Did you have anything to do with this medical centre?' Elizabeth asked after more slowly turning time had passed.

'What makes you ask?'

She smiled. 'The main general ward is called the Trakas Ward, plus in the waiting room there's a plaque on the wall with your name on it.'

He laughed with as much humour as he could muster. 'The islanders raised the bulk of the money for the building. I just paid the remainder and gave the cash for the equipment.'

Her eyes widened. 'All of it?'

He shrugged. 'Diadonus is my home. My family are fortunate enough to be able to afford any medical intervention we need. The rest of the islanders aren't so lucky.'

'Did the rest of your family contribute?' Elizabeth was awed at his generosity.

'Yanis and Katerina made a donation.'

'Your parents?'

He raised a brow that quite clearly said she'd asked a stupid question. 'My family have lived here for generations but have never contributed to life here. Yanis and I wanted to do things differently. Loukas is the first Trakas child to attend the local school and not to go private. His parents wanted him to have friends on his doorstep and not have to fly hundreds of miles for a play date. We have enormous wealth and it's time we started putting something back into the place we call home.'

'How did your parents take the decision to educate him here?'

'Badly.'

That one word was enough. She'd only met Mirela the once but Elizabeth could well imagine her disdain at her only grandchild being educated with 'normal' children. It would have been a huge black mark against Yanis and Katerina's names.

But it was a welcome reminder that, despite their addictions, Yanis and Katerina loved their son and had done their best for him. She just hoped they both recovered enough to do their best for him in the future too.

If they didn't…

Well, Xander would always be there for him, loving him as fiercely as if he were his own.

But all this was speculation. They had the court case to get through first. Mirela and Dragan *couldn't* win. They couldn't. If she had to pledge her whole life to stop that happening she would give it gladly.

Elizabeth was so lost in her thoughts that at first she didn't notice the nurse come back in the room.

She was smiling as she spoke to them.

Xander got to his feet, relief all over his face. 'The operation's done and Loukas is in the recovery ward. He's expected to start waking any moment.'

'It was a success?'

He nodded. 'They're confident.'

She smiled and expelled air she hadn't realised she'd been holding.

Xander wished Loukas a good night and closed the bedroom door behind him. The nanny had moved into the next room so she could keep an eye on him throughout the night.

Elizabeth was waiting for him in the corridor.

'I have a confession to make,' she blurted.

He studied her exhausted face, wondering what could cause her to look and sound so tense. They'd both spent the night at the hospital with Loukas and the majority of the day there waiting for him to be discharged. He doubted either of them had got more than a couple of hours' sleep in all. 'What's wrong?'

'I pranged your car.' She sounded so miserable he had to bite back a laugh.

'Is that all? I thought you were going to tell me something really bad. Are you hurt?' She didn't look hurt, only tired. Her gorgeous curls were starting to frizz.

'It happened when I was driving it back from the hospital.'

He'd driven himself there in his Lotus, doing the return journey with Loukas beside him and Elizabeth following them. Now he thought about it, he remembered losing her and getting back a good ten minutes before her. He'd been so concerned with making sure his nephew was comfortable he'd forgotten all about it.

'Did you hit another car?'

'No. But there's a barrier along the coastline with a fresh dent in it.' She stared at the ground. 'The road was really narrow and there was a truck coming towards me. I didn't think there was enough room for the two of us so I pulled over to let him pass and scraped the barrier.'

'As long as you're not hurt, I couldn't care less.' Thinking of her hurt or injured...

'But it was your Porsche.'

He wrapped his arms around her and drew her to him, swallowing back the constriction in his throat. 'It's a car and I'm sure it's repairable. If not, it's replaceable. You're not.'

She never had been...

She rested her head against his chest. 'Will your parents know about Loukas's arm?'

'Probably. They seem to know most things. It doesn't matter. It was an accident.'

'If they try and twist it I'll put them straight.' She said it with such venom he was taken aback.

The events of the past two days had opened up an understanding between his wife and nephew. A bond. Loukas had put aside his fears and opened his heart to her, something Xander knew had taken an enormous amount of courage from the little boy.

And Elizabeth had opened her heart to Loukas, something that had taken an enormous amount of courage from *her*.

Thinking of his investigator's report on her, he now considered it with a fresh perspective.

The life she'd lived had, on the surface, been glamorous and filled with friends if not lovers. But all her friends predated their first time on St Francis. Apart from her employees, for whom she clearly retained a deep affection, she hadn't made a single new true friend in a decade.

Was it possible she hadn't dated in that time too?

He didn't know how he felt about that possibility. The reasoning for it led to too many different avenues, none of which sat comfortably with him.

If she didn't date, how could she ever be a mother?

They'd spoken of having kids together. Hell, they'd even chosen names for them: Samuel, Giannis, Imogen and Rebecca.

Where had *that* memory come from? And why did his heart twist with it?

He was comfortable with the idea of never being a father. He had Loukas in his life. That was enough.

'Do you want to get something to eat?' he asked, more to break the darkness of his thoughts than out of hunger.

Her chest jerked against his. 'I'm so tired I'd probably fall asleep in it.'

He drew back to take her face in his hands. 'What do you say we take a shower together and go to bed? Stay the night with me.'

Xander knew he was being selfish asking this of her but, after the stress of the past two days and the additional stress of the coming day, he didn't want to be alone with his own thoughts. Elizabeth had a way of soothing the stress so it was more a dull ache than a thudding beat.

Besides, he was sick of them sneaking between the two rooms. They weren't furtive teenagers. They both knew where they stood with each other. Neither of them would mistake comforting the other through the night with anything more meaningful.

Her amber eyes held his as if she was searching for something. Then a small smile curled her lips and she nodded.

They slept in a tangle of limbs until his alarm clock woke them.

It was time to go to court.

CHAPTER TWELVE

XANDER'S KNUCKLES WERE WHITE.

When Elizabeth met his gaze, she realised it wasn't nerves causing it but contained anger.

This was a court battle he had no intention of losing.

It was a battle she was determined to help him win.

In the courthouse they were taken to a private hearing room with Xander's team of lawyers.

His parents were already there with their own team of lawyers.

It was the first time she'd met Dragan, his father. First glances did not inspire optimism.

Like his wife and son, Dragan was impeccably groomed. A little shorter than his wife, he kept himself in good shape and a thick mop of dark hair on his head made him appear younger than his years. It occurred to her that it was too dark and thick to be natural, and she had to bite her cheek not to laugh. It was the only thing she could find to laugh about.

They'd left Loukas behind, a day of watching

movies and eating ice cream with Rachael on his agenda, oblivious that his future would be determined that day. If his grandparents won, he would be uprooted from his home and everyone he loved and forced to live, probably permanently, with people he barely knew.

If Xander won, he would soon be able to return to his own home with his father, if not his mother. If Xander won, Loukas would always be able to call his uncle's home *his* home too.

Xander's love for his nephew was not in doubt. It saddened her that he wouldn't have a child of his own. He would be a brilliant father but he had no intention of making a proper marriage and so had discounted having a child. Just as she had done...

But now was not the time to think of this.

Mirela and Dragan had written a statement. As Xander had predicted when they'd discussed the case, they were portraying themselves as innocent victims who'd been deliberately pushed out of their only grandson's life by his addicted parents. Their second son, Xander, was an enabler. If he cared about his nephew he would have insisted his brother go into rehab much sooner and it was a sign of his short-sightedness due to his inherently selfish nature that this had only happened when he'd realised his parents weren't prepared to be bystanders in their grandson's life any more.

Elizabeth watched Xander's reaction as this statement was read out. She was quite certain that if she put a pin in him he would explode with rage.

She wanted to explode with rage too. How dared his parents tell such lies?

Then it was time for Xander's statement. He'd spent hours drafting it and a copy was handed to the judge. Instead of one of his lawyers reading from it, Xander rose to speak for himself, without notes.

He laid the facts out in chronological detail, starting with his and Yanis's own wretched childhood at the hand of their parents and explaining that it was for this reason Yanis and Katerina had been determined to protect their only child from the influence of two people incapable of showing a child affection. The statement ended with a request for common sense to prevail and a copy of the report from the facility where Yanis was being treated—successfully—was produced for all to read. All being well, Yanis would be home in a month.

His parents had no legal or moral basis to take away a loved child from the people who had cared for him since his birth. If Yanis and Katerina felt they were unable to care for their own child any more, then they should be given the chance to determine who could do so in their absence, just as they'd done in this circumstance when they'd left Loukas in Xander's care.

'That only goes to show how the drugs and alcohol have affected their judgement,' Mirela said. 'Our youngest son is an exceptional businessman, we concede that, but he doesn't know the first thing about raising a child. He's a pleasure seeker, a sex addict who has brought shame and scandal on the

Trakas name, just as his brother has with his sub-stance addiction. Children need two parents. My daughter-in-law is very ill; Yanis is not fit to care for Loukas on his own. The wife Xander has pro-duced is a stooge, brought here so you forget he's not fit to raise a child—if you allow Xander to continue his guardianship, she will disappear as soon as the paperwork is signed.'

The lawyer to Elizabeth's left, who was translat-ing for her, explained what she'd said.

She clenched her hands into fists, her brain burn-ing.

If she weren't in a courthouse she might very well launch herself at Mirela and scratch her face.

'Am I allowed to say something?' she asked.

The lawyer asked the judge, who nodded her con-sent.

Speaking slowly so her words could be translated, Elizabeth said, 'Forgive me my lack of preparation but I didn't expect to speak today.'

The judge nodded her understanding.

'My husband is not the man the papers have por-trayed him to be. Even if he was, it doesn't affect his relationship with his nephew. Loukas adores him and respects his authority over him. Xander is his one constant. He's comfortable and happy with him, but he doesn't know his grandparents. They're strang-ers to him...'

'Strangers because Yanis has never let us be in his life!' Dragan interjected heatedly.

'And that's because Yanis doesn't want his son

under your influence.' She focused on staying calm, knowing if she were to raise her voice any valid points the judge might think she was making would be nullified. 'Yanis has addictions, there's no disputing that, but it's hardly surprising when you consider he never felt you, his parents, loved him and that to receive your approval he had to marry a woman he didn't love when he was twenty.

'The only reason Xander hasn't turned out the same is because he watched his brother go through it first and determined not to be like him. To do that he had to defy you and all the plans you'd made for him, and you have never forgiven him for that, and you've never forgiven him for taking control of the business from you, and you've never forgiven Yanis for raising his son differently from how you think he should be raised. Because that's what this is about, surely? Revenge on your sons. If it was about what's best for Loukas we wouldn't be sitting here.'

Now she looked directly at the judge. 'I don't know if Yanis will stay clean from his addictions and I don't know if Katerina will recover, but I do know that Xander will be there for them both and, most importantly, he will love and care for Loukas as if he were his own.'

Although there were thousands more words she wanted to say, Elizabeth figured she'd gone far enough. She could feel Xander's eyes boring into her but didn't dare look at him. Would he be angry with her for speaking out? She couldn't have kept her mouth shut a moment longer if she'd tried.

The rest of the hearing flew by until they were excused by the judge and filed out while she contemplated her judgement.

'Let's get something to eat,' Xander said in an undertone that, she was relieved to note, didn't sound angry. If anything he sounded pleased.

As soon as they were outside the courthouse, he grabbed hold of her and kissed her, a huge passionate kiss that took her by such surprise she clung to the lapels of his jacket to stay upright.

'You are brilliant,' he said when he finally unlocked his mouth from hers.

'You're not angry with me?'

He shook his head, incredulity in his eyes. 'Elizabeth… What you said…'

'All I said was the truth, as I see it.'

He kissed her again then led her to a cramped restaurant around the corner from the courthouse. No sooner had they been shown to a table when his parents strolled in. They took one look at him and Elizabeth and walked straight back out.

'I think you were right that this is all about revenge,' he said after they'd ordered.

'Having met your mother, it was the only thing that made sense to me. You refused to do as they wanted when you reached adulthood *and* wrested control of their own company from them.'

He'd told her the story of the deal he'd made with them for control of the business while Loukas had been sleeping in the hospital.

'They taught me too well.'

'When this is over, you should make your peace with them,' she said softly.

That killed his good mood. 'To find peace one has to acquire forgiveness. They don't deserve that.'

Her gaze was steady on his. 'Maybe not, but hasn't there been enough revenge and punishment within your family?'

His parents had neglected their sons, forced Yanis into a loveless marriage and played a part in Ana's state of mind before her death. Who could forgive that?

In return, Xander had taken control of their company and put himself in a position of power over them. As far as revenge and punishment went, he'd hit them where it hurt the most.

And then they'd gone for custody of Loukas. A never-ending circle of revenge.

He evaded the question. 'Have you forgiven your parents for the way they treated you?'

She pursed her lips thoughtfully before answering. 'I've lost my anger towards them. I don't see them all that much but the time I do spend with them isn't filled with resentment. I've let that go. If that's forgiveness then I guess I have forgiven them.' Her amber eyes looked up at him, shining. 'And I've forgiven you for how you treated me all those years ago.'

Everything constricted in him. 'I really am sorry for how I ended things. I thought I was doing the right thing.'

Walking away from Elizabeth had been one of the only selfless things he'd ever done in his life.

'You had the best of intentions,' she conceded. 'It's how you carried it out that left much to be desired.'

He sighed. 'Everything was so intense between us, like a hundred holiday romances rolled into one. When I knew I had to end it I knew it would be kinder to sever it in one stroke rather than string you along.'

'Just answer me one thing: if Ana hadn't died, would you have taken me home?'

'I don't know. Probably. But her death was the wake-up call I needed. You were a different woman then. If you'd come home with me we would never have lasted. My parents—my mother especially—would have crushed you. We've both changed since then.'

'We didn't have a chance, did we?' she said sadly.

He grimaced, thinking how right she was. 'You forgive me for then but what about now? Can you forgive me for blackmailing you?'

'And forcing me to lose my business?' she added drily.

'For that too.'

Her eyes melted before him and then she gave a smile of such beauty, light seemed to radiate from her. 'I'm getting there.'

He took her hand in his and brought it to his lips.

He'd never asked for or sought Elizabeth's forgiveness before but now he had it, it felt as if a weight he hadn't known was there had been lifted from him.

* * *

It was to their immense relief that the judge threw out Mirela and Dragan's custody claim. Xander insisted on taking Elizabeth out to celebrate.

After kissing Loukas goodnight, the little boy blissfully unaware how close his life had come to being ruined, she went to her room to change while Xander put him to bed.

As the evening was a touch chilly, she settled on a pair of skinny jeans and a sweeping blush top with sequins around the neckline and hem. Ready before Xander, she turned her laptop on. The first thing that flashed up when it had loaded was the gossip site she used as her home page, mostly so she could keep a watchful eye on her matches. Its main headline picture was of Dante and Piper, dressed to the nines, gazing into each other's eyes with complete adoration. There was no way it could be faked.

This was the last thing she'd expected. Dante Mancini in love?

She smiled as she imagined how Piper must be feeling and was glad she'd held back the warnings she'd wanted to give the sweet Australian about protecting her heart.

When this was all over between her and Xander, she would give Piper a call and hear for herself how she was getting on.

When this was all over...?

Blinking the thought away, she wondered how the other two Casanovas were faring with their matches. Although she hadn't actually matched Zayn with

Amalia she had seen enough to think there was a big enough spark between them to see them through. Benjamin and Julianna, she was convinced, were the real deal.

It occurred to her that only a week ago she would have been silently furious at how things had turned out for them. *You fools,* she would have wanted to yell, *don't you realise you're going to get your hearts broken?*

But it was with her own heart thundering that she realised she no longer felt like that. Love didn't have to end with heartbreak and misery.

When this was all over...

Her heart ready to explode through her ribcage, the enormous truth she'd been hiding from herself smacked her round the face.

She wasn't ready for this to be over. She didn't want to say goodbye to Xander. Not yet. Not ever...

By his own admission they'd both changed. *Could* there be a proper future for them?

There was a light rap on the adjoining door and then Xander appeared through it. 'Ready to go...?' His brow furrowed. 'Are you okay?'

She nodded and closed the lid of her laptop, trying to get a handle on her thoughts. 'Yes and yes. Is Loukas asleep?'

'Out like a light.'

Hand in hand, they strolled out of the back of the villa and down to Xander's private beach where his yacht was waiting on the jetty. From there they sailed to Mykonos where, Xander insisted, the best fish restaurant in Greece was located. And he was right. They shared a seafood platter filled with the most delicious jumbo prawns, whitebait, calamari, octopus and mussels, served with salad, dips and pitta. They also drank their way through a carafe of white wine and two shots each of ouzo.

It was the best evening Elizabeth could remember, certainly the best since the day she'd pledged to spend the rest of her life with Xander.

Would things have been different if they'd first met as adults? she wondered for the tenth time that evening, as he regaled her with an old story of his mother getting the better of an Italian cosmetics company. They'd been competing for prime floor space in a Europe-wide department store chain. Mirela had won the space, despite offering less than the Italians.

Listening to him speak about his parents, she quite understood why he would continue working with them. Between them and with Xander at the helm they were a formidable team.

It was, as he'd said a few weeks ago, only as human beings that his parents were useless.

And listening to him, seeing him unwind and relax…it was like being with the Xander of old.

Watching him via press cuttings over the years, when he was always presented in an impeccable business suit, never a hair out of place, his shoes never less than shiny, his expression never less than inscrutable, she'd forgotten how fun he could be. But he'd liked having things his own way then too, she remembered. If he'd wanted something to happen he'd made it happen, including the fast track of their marriage. When he'd proposed to her she'd been convinced it would take weeks to get everything in place, not days as Xander had ensured.

He'd been formidable even then but she'd been so in love that this side of him had never really registered on her radar. She'd only cared about his fun and passionate sides.

Now she knew the whole man, the good, the bad and the ugly. The real Xander, not the idealised image he'd portrayed to her on their sunny Caribbean paradise. Not the idealised image *she'd* formed him into being to fill the massive gap in her heart.

And as she drained the last of her wine, she realised she loved him even more now than she had then.

Yes. She could admit it. She loved him. And as he gazed at her, the expression in his eyes the same as when he'd looked at her a decade ago, her hopeful heart couldn't stop her thinking that he might feel the same about her.

Nothing was said about their future. Life carried on as before but with a lightness of heart that made Elizabeth feel she was walking on air.

Her days were spent scribbling in her notebook—she was on her sixth one now—either on the beach or, if it was too cold, in the infinity room. The sound of the infinity pool was almost as soothing as the sea but the underfloor heating kept her warm. Now that she'd admitted to herself that she loved him, it was as if her heart had bloomed and the storyline for her script came pouring out of her, so fast she struggled to keep up with it. Once she had the whole thing plotted she would get the actual script written on her laptop.

Should she find an agent? she wondered.

Get it written first and then think about the next step.

Yet no matter how deeply into her storyline she sank, she still spent the hours Xander worked with a watchful eye on the time for when he returned.

Such was the bubble of bliss she'd cocooned herself in that it came as something of a shock when Xander returned home a month after the court case with the news that Yanis was coming home.

Leaving Loukas, whose arm was mending beautifully, in her care, Xander flew to America to collect him.

As she'd successfully pushed this event to the back of her mind, Elizabeth was suddenly terrified of the implications of Yanis's return. To get through it she had to keep herself busy. Luckily it was the weekend so she and Loukas spent most of it together building sandcastles, watching movies and playing hide and seek. He was a gorgeous child and, now he'd accepted her, she'd discovered his funny, mischievous side. She would miss him when it was time for her to leave…

But she didn't want to think about leaving. It was taking everything to hold back the tears as it was.

This was what she wanted. She wanted to be here, with Xander, creating their own family.

There were times when he made love to her or when she caught him looking at her in an unguarded moment when she thought he *had* to feel the same but just because she'd forgiven him for the past didn't mean she could forget. She'd thought he loved her a decade ago and she'd been wrong then. She could easily be wrong now.

It was thus with a certain amount of trepidation mingling with the excitement of him being home that she saw Xander's car appear on the driveway late on the Sunday afternoon.

Loukas spotted it too and went tearing out to meet them while she hung back sedately, practising her calm face, trying to forget that as soon as Xander and Yanis came up with a legally binding agreement for Xander to be guardian in Yanis's absence, her agreement with Xander would be over. She'd be free to go home.

But would he want her to stay? That was the million-dollar question.

It was somewhat of a shock to actually meet Yanis. Like Xander he was tall but that was the only similarity. His handsome face was gaunt, his hair, a darker shade than his brother's, receding. He looked exactly like what he was: a recovering drug addict.

He came straight to her and gave her a tight hug. 'It is a pleasure to meet you,' he said in a raspy voice. 'Xander has told me what you've done. I thank you for everything.'

'It's lovely to meet you too,' she murmured, pleasurably taken aback at such a warm welcome.

They kissed on both cheeks then chaos ensued. All the household staff appeared wanting to welcome Yanis home. Some, like Rachael the nanny, normally worked for Yanis directly in his home, Xander having seconded them in his brother's absence. Loukas ran around like a hyperactive bee, so much so that Xander had to warn him that he was in danger of breaking his arm again, which slowed him down for all of half a minute.

It was a happy day that culminated in a celebratory dinner. When it was time for Loukas to go to bed, Elizabeth excused herself.

'You're going to bed already?' Xander asked in surprise.

'I've got a headache,' she lied. She sensed Yanis had found the day overwhelming and needed some space. Alone with his brother he could relax and not put on a happy front for her benefit.

Xander had the feeling she wasn't being truthful but let it go. He and Yanis had discussed many things on the flight back from America and during the detour they'd taken in Athens, but there were still things to talk about in more depth. He would deal with that and then he would deal with his wife.

'I'll see you soon,' he said, tugging her down for a kiss.

She brushed her hand over his hair with a smile and disappeared.

'She's lovely,' Yanis said when they were alone.

'She is,' he agreed. He'd told Yanis everything. His brother hadn't been able to show a modicum of shock at their parents' actions but his eyes had blazed with glee when Xander relayed how Elizabeth had decimated them in front of the judge.

She had been magnificent.

'Loukas seems very taken with her.'

'They understand each other. She's very protective of him.'

'She's protective of you too.'

'Is she?'

Yanis stared at him as if he were an idiot.

But it got him thinking. Elizabeth was not the woman he'd married a decade ago. The sweet, loving woman he'd met was still there but with added spine. And what a spine it was! Whenever he thought of the off-the-cuff speech she'd made to the judge, his heart would swell with pride.

Now his brother was back and everything was being sorted, he knew their arrangement was at an end. He'd imagined at the beginning that when this moment came he would help her pack her bags but now…he felt different.

CHAPTER THIRTEEN

A FEW HOURS LATER Xander found Elizabeth reading in his bed.

She welcomed him with a lazy smile.

'How's your head?' He climbed onto the bed beside her.

She turned to face him and planted a kiss on his lips. 'Fine. How's Yanis? He was looking a little overwhelmed with everything.'

'He's getting there.' Wrapping his arms around her so her head was snuggled against his chest, he said, 'We've had a good talk about things. I didn't mention it before because Loukas was there but we went to see Katerina earlier. They've both agreed to name me as legal guardian should they ever be unable to care for Loukas themselves again.'

'Do you think it will come to that again?' she asked softly.

'I hope not. Katerina's looking better but she still won't admit she has a problem. Right now she can't drink but they're talking about letting her go home in a couple of weeks. That's when we'll know if she's got a mind to kick the alcohol.'

'Will she come back to Diadonus?'

'No, she'll live in their apartment in Athens. It'll be better for her there as she'll have quicker access to the hospital if she needs it. The medical centre here is good but it doesn't cater for everything. Her sister's going to stay with her. Yanis and Loukas will visit regularly but will stay here for a few weeks while Yanis gets used to civilisation again.'

'Fingers crossed everything works out for them all.'

'I feel more hopeful than I did a couple of months ago. Yanis is resigning from the Timos board. I've been telling him for years to do it but he was worried he'd feel even more like a failure for it. Now he can see it's for the best. He doesn't know what he'll do but without the pressure and stress of a job he hates and having to deal with our parents on a daily basis, he'll have a much stronger footing to stay clean.'

She sighed into him and curved her arm a little tighter around his waist.

'I can't predict the future and, while I am hopeful things will work out for the best, I'm not going to lie that I think it will be easy. Which is where you come in.'

Her head shifted, her curls tickling his chin. 'Me?'

'Yanis will need a lot of support. He's dealing with major upheavals. There's no guarantee he won't slip up on occasions. Loukas is going to need a lot of support too.'

She didn't answer, so he carried on. 'I know we said that once we'd sorted out a legal agreement for

Loukas to be in my care that you could go back to New York, but I would like you to reconsider.'

'You want me to stay?'

'Just for a few more months while things settle themselves down. Loukas has grown very fond of you. It will be good for him to have another constant in his life.'

She sat up, holding the sheets to her chest. 'That's all you require? A few more months?'

'Maybe longer. Let's take it one day at a time.'

To Xander's mind, this was the perfect solution. The chemistry between him and Elizabeth burned as strongly as ever. They'd resolved their differences and were happy together. He liked her being around and she obviously liked being there too. It seemed ludicrous to end it because of an arbitrary cut-off point they'd decided on before they'd become lovers again. If he was being completely honest with himself, he wasn't ready to let her go. Not yet.

Her face didn't give anything away. 'And then what? You decide everything's hunky-dory and send me back to New York?'

'I thought you'd be happy to stay a bit longer. You like it here, don't you?' To prove his point, he leaned into her neck and nipped it. 'And we can continue having amazing sex.'

She shoved him away. 'Anyone can have good sex.'

'Says the voice of experience?' It still rankled that he knew nothing of her sexual history in the years they'd been apart.

He waited for her to smile or make a quip but her lips pursed together and she contemplated him for an age before saying quietly, 'Level with me, Xander. What are your feelings for me?'

'Well...' He racked his brains, ignoring the alarm bells suddenly playing like a siren in his gut. 'You're beautiful, caring, witty, gutsy, and have the most fabulous hair, and you're amazingly responsive in bed.'

She didn't give even the flicker of a smile. 'And how do I assimilate in your world? Do you think I fit in now?'

'You fit in much better than I thought you would.' He caught a curl in his fingers and gently tugged at it. 'We suit each other very well.'

'You make it sound so romantic.'

'We did romance once and look where that got us.'

'We were little more than children then.'

He dropped her curl and twisted to look more clearly at her. 'What are you trying to say?'

'Nothing.'

But by the set look on her face it was clearly something.

'Talk to me. Tell me what's on your mind.'

She gave a slow nod, her eyes narrowed. 'Okay. But first let me make sure I've got what you're proposing straight. You want me to stay for a few more months while things settle down with your family, and then you're happy for me to go back to New York and carry on with my life without you?'

'That's a little colder than I would describe it but

essentially, yes. Think of it as an extended vacation with excellent sex thrown into the mix.'

'And then we go our separate ways with a kiss and fond memories?'

'Exactly right. I'm happy to transfer the thirty million into your account now,' he added as an afterthought.

She flinched, then stared at him for another long pause. 'You know, for someone so sensitive and thoughtful to his family's needs, you can be a real insensitive bastard.'

Her words landed like a punch to his gut. 'What are you talking about?'

Her face now white, she flung the sheets off, jumped off the bed, and went through the adjoining door to her own room.

'What's the matter with you?' he demanded to know when she still hadn't answered his question.

She threw her dressing room door open. 'Where, at any point in your investigator's report on me, did it say anything about me being free and easy with my body and indulging in pointless affairs?'

'I'm not suggesting a pointless affair, Elizabeth. I just don't see why it has to end now when you staying here will be beneficial…'

'To Loukas,' she finished for him, pulling a pair of panties on. 'Where all I get out of it is *good sex*.' She grabbed a T-shirt off a shelf and shrugged it on. 'Where do my feelings come into it? What about what I want?'

'You've told me what you want. You don't believe in love and relationships.'

'And why is that?' She put her hands on her hips, eyes blazing with what he could see was incandescent fury. 'I'll tell you why—it's because you completely screwed me up when you abandoned me five days after marrying me, that's why!'

Now she pulled a pair of jeans off the rail. 'You broke my heart. Did you know that? Completely smashed it. I told myself my parents' marriage and the loathing they had for each other was just a case of bad pairing and that true love did exist, but you showed me how very wrong I was. You want to know how many men I've slept with since you left me? None. Not a single affair. You destroyed my faith in *everything* and you destroyed my hopes of love so completely that I turned my back on the life I'd always wanted.'

Xander stared at her, stunned at her outburst. She hadn't been with anyone else…?

'I thought we had a meeting of minds when it came to relationships,' he said, breathing heavily, working hard to get his thoughts into order.

She fastened the buttons of her jeans then gazed at the ceiling. 'My feelings have changed.' Then her face contorted again and the brief moment of calm was shattered. 'I don't want to be convenient. I don't want to have an affair because it's for the best. I want to be wanted for me. I never had that when I was growing up—I was always just an asset to be fought over. I wasn't loved for *me*, I was a weapon to be used. I thought I'd found love ten years ago with you but then you dumped me because I wasn't good enough.'

'You *were* good enough.' Xander swore under his breath, trying his hardest to keep his temper. 'We've been over this time and time again. What more do you want me to say? I couldn't bring you back with me. You would have been destroyed.'

'You didn't even *try*,' she cried. 'If you'd loved me then you would have fought for me. You could have moved to New York with me. You haven't cared what your parents thought about you for a long time, your brother would have understood, he might even have made the move with you! But no, you didn't do any of that and I'll tell you why, it's because that bloody business meant more to you than I did. It still means more than anything else...'

'That's crap,' he cut in heatedly.

'Really? Then why aren't Yanis and Katerina putting themselves out of their misery and getting a divorce? It's because of the potential cost to the business, isn't it? As long as Timos is okay, everything else can go to hell. You can have an affair with me now and pretend to the world we have a normal marriage without consequences because I now "fit" into your world. You don't have to make *any* concessions.'

His ears were ringing, the room losing its focus. 'You're talking nonsense.'

'Am I? I was prepared to give up everything for you because I loved you, but you...' She shook her head with loathing. 'You weren't prepared to lose your place in the company for anything as pathetic as love. Well, you're the pathetic one and I deserve so much more. I want it all, Xander. Spending time with Loukas and you has made me see how much I've denied myself and what I've been missing out on. I want a family of my own and if you tell me you want it too then we could have it because guess what? I still love you.'

Her words sent him reeling. 'You do?'

'Yep! But I am not prepared to waste another ten years of my life pining for a man who doesn't feel the same way, so I will ask you one more time— what are your feelings for me? And don't give me any crap about me being witty or any other such garbage. I want to know your real feelings or I walk out this minute.'

Xander was trapped. He didn't know what he was expected to say, his head spinning from her declaration of love. And she wanted a family with him...?

But it hadn't sounded like a real declaration. More an angry outburst, something she disliked saying as much as he disliked hearing it.

'You know how I feel about marriage. I've made that perfectly clear. I should never have married you in the first place.'

'So why did you?'

'Because I was young and stupid.'

She flinched.

'I'm sorry, Elizabeth, but you want the truth so I'm giving it to you. My feelings haven't changed. I don't want to make a commitment that ties me to one person's side for the rest of my life. I like you a lot, you know that. I care for you. But we've both seen how destructive tying yourself to one person can be. I don't believe in for ever and you *know* you don't believe in it either.'

She stared at him for an inordinate amount of time, her eyes flashing with fury and pain, but mostly fury. 'You can stick your offer where the sun doesn't shine. I'm going home.'

'Why? Because I'm not prepared to make a false promise?' Had she not listened to anything he'd said?

'No. Because your feelings for me aren't strong enough for you to take that leap of faith. Can you arrange for your crew to fly me to Athens, or do I have to steal a boat?'

She couldn't be serious. Things were great as they were between them. Why was she trying to spoil things now? Where had all this come from?

'Sleep on it. You'll feel differently in the morning. It's been a long, emotional day...'

'Do not tell me how I'm feeling or how I should be feeling. I want to go home, so are you going to help me or not?'

He thought quickly, which was hard with all the blood roaring in his head. 'I'll get them to fly you to Athens after breakfast and I'll have the jet ready to take you to New York.'

Whatever she said, she would feel differently in the morning. They could discuss it properly then, when she wasn't feeling so irrational about the situation, when she could see that taking it one day at a time wasn't a rejection but simply taking it one day at a time.

She steamed past him and opened the adjoining door. 'You can leave me alone now.'

He looked at her one last time.

'You'll feel differently in the morning,' he repeated.

The lock clicked behind him.

Xander opened his eyes, surprised to see his bedside clock reading nine a.m. He'd still been awake at five, certain he would never be able to fall asleep.

He felt sick, and not just in his stomach. Everything inside him felt twisted.

He staggered out of bed and knocked on the adjoining door. Sighing when there was no reply and the door remained steadfastly locked, he showered then headed to the infinity room for his breakfast, bracing himself for a cold shoulder.

Yanis and Loukas were at the table, already eating.

They both looked at him accusingly as he entered the room.

'What?'

'Elizabeth's gone.'

'To the beach?' She took a long walk most days. He'd put some shoes on and go find her.

'Home,' said Loukas. 'She woke me up to say goodbye.' Then he smiled. 'She's given me her email address and phone number. Daddy says I can call her whenever I want.'

The last words were faint as Xander was already heading back down the stairs.

Her main bedroom door was unlocked. He pushed it open and immediately thought they were playing with him. Her bed was neatly made and all her cosmetics and perfumes sat on the dressing table as they had done for over a month. Her dressing room was still filled with her clothes.

All her stuff was there. She couldn't have gone. They must be messing with...

And then he realised what *was* missing and his heart stopped. Elizabeth's laptop was gone. In a frenzy he opened drawers and doors, looking for the copious amounts of stationery she had filled them with in her time on Diadonus. They were all gone too.

Elizabeth put her case in the overhead locker and settled herself into the economy seat she'd purchased three minutes before the desk closed and thanked whoever was looking down and helping her that she'd managed to get a seat on the day's only flight to New York.

Gazing out of the window, she couldn't help strain her eyes for something out of the ordinary, some sign...

She'd done exactly the same thing ten years ago on her flight back to New York from St Francis. She'd hoped desperately for a miracle, for Xander to suddenly appear and tell her it had all been a mistake, that he was sorry and he did love her and they would spend the rest of their lives together.

There hadn't been anything then and nor was there anything now.

She'd caught the early morning ferry from Diadonus Town harbour and watched the island she'd come to think of as home disappear until it became a dot and then, nothing. Four hours later they'd docked in Piraeus and she'd been helpless to stop her eyes from scanning everywhere for a sign of him; if he'd wanted to, he could have easily beaten her there.

That miracle will never happen. It didn't happen ten years ago and it won't happen now. Forget him. Carry on with your life. Forget this ever happened.

Yet for all the stern words she aimed at herself, she was helpless to stop the tears pouring down her face as the plane taxied down the runway. As they became airborne and she stared like a masochist through blurred eyes for her last look at a city she had come to love, she had to stuff her fist into her mouth to prevent the pain from screaming itself out.

CHAPTER FOURTEEN

XANDER FINGERED THE NOTEBOOK one of his staff had just given to him.

It had fallen down the back of Elizabeth's dresser, lying there unnoticed while she'd gathered together the few possessions she'd arrived with.

She'd been gone for four days now. He'd felt every minute of it.

Curiosity overcame him and he turned the cover. As he took it all in it struck him that he'd never seen her handwriting before. He'd only seen her signature on their wedding licence ten years ago. The only way to describe it was neat and curvy. Not that he could see much writing on the first few pages—mostly it was filled with doodles; flowers, single eyes with thick long lashes, stiletto shoes and…teapots?

He flicked through a few more pages of doodles over which more of her curvy handwriting appeared, random sentences that didn't make sense until, after half an hour immersed in it, he realised it all connected and that she'd been working on the kernels of a storyline for a script. These were all her initial thoughts but he could see the broad strokes of what it would be. A tale of a fork in a road, one fork leading to love and redemption, the other leading to loneliness and hell.

Elizabeth had no idea how many miles she'd walked but when she found herself near the entrance of the Central Park Zoo, she figured at least four. Despite living in the city all her life, she'd only been to the zoo once, on a field trip in junior high.

She'd loved it there and had always hoped one of her parents would take her. After a while she'd stopped asking. Neither of them had any interest in her unless it involved getting one up on the other. Unfortunately for her small self, that hadn't included days out at the zoo. And then she'd grown up and spent a decade way too busy to even think of going there.

She paid the entrance fee and opened her guide map. If she started with the penguins and the seabirds, she could do a whole loop of the place. How could anyone fail to be happy at the sight of penguins?

She could.

Nothing lifted her mood, not the penguins or the thickly furred snow monkeys, not even the lemurs in the tropic zone who were showing off in spectacular fashion for their delighted audience.

Maybe that was why her mood wouldn't lift. She was surrounded by families; mothers, fathers and children, all reminding her of what could have been.

She would come back on a weekday when families would be at a minimum.

Once out of the tropic zone the chill in the air really hit her. The clouds were thick above her and within minutes a snowflake landed on her nose.

Normally she loved the snow but it was hard to appreciate it when she was pining for a sunny Greek island thousands of miles away. Only the island though, she assured herself. And Loukas. She missed him very much. Xander...

She would not think of him.

Wanting coffee and to go home, she headed for the exit. The gift shop winked at her.

After a moment's indecision, she crunched through the falling snow to it.

As she'd known there would be, the shop had notebooks galore.

Her cell rang from her purse. About to reach for it, she remembered there was nothing important she needed to answer it for. Her time was her own. She had thirty million dollars in her bank account and a big wide world to explore and write about.

For the first time in a week she felt a glimmer of light amid the darkness in her heart.

The world was hers to do as she wanted. She was *rich*. She could form her own production company and option her own scripts.

While none of this meant anything to her right now, at some point in the future, when the pain began to ease, she knew it would mean a great deal.

Wherever life took her, she would just have to make a point of avoiding Greece and its islands.

She paid for five notebooks and left the gift shop feeling more positive than she had in days.

She'd thrown her toys out of the pram the last time Xander had broken her heart and she was *not* going to do the same thing again.

Love *did* exist. It *did*. And maybe one day, when she least expected it, it would come to her and she would hug it close and cherish it with everything she had.

Xander's face flashed in her mind again.

She missed him. She ached for him. She would never see him again.

But she wouldn't throw her life away because of it. Not again.

The snow fell thick and fast around her but she wasn't tempted to jump on a bus or train or grab a cab. The snow was invigorating.

As she walked the four miles back, she was aware of her cell continuing to ring but by now all she wanted was to get home. She would deal with anything then.

Feeling like an Eskimo, she turned onto Seventh Avenue. A figure at the bottom of the stairway to the front door of her apartment block made her pause. She squinted through the snow to see more clearly.

Time itself stood still. Elizabeth couldn't move, was only vaguely aware of people bustling around her.

During all the walks she'd taken since she'd been

home she'd thought she'd seen him a dozen times or more but not once had she really believed it was him. It was only her pining heart taking its time in accepting reality.

This time it really was him.

She forced her legs to keep going.

By the time she reached him she'd squashed the burst of joy, stamped it into a box and locked it away.

Yet up close, seeing him standing there, his long navy blue overcoat sodden with snow, the tip of his nose red with cold, snowflakes on his brows and lashes...

Oh, she had to try so damned hard not to throw herself into his arms.

She had to try even harder to get her throat to move but then she couldn't think of anything to say and, suddenly terrified she was going to cry, stalked past him up the steps that had been mercifully gritted, and unlocked the front door.

Stamping the snow off her boots, she grabbed her mail and then walked to the end of the passageway and unlocked her apartment door.

Xander stayed beside her the whole time. Neither of them made an attempt to speak.

Once she'd closed the door she put her back to it and faced him. 'Why are you here?'

Xander took in the tiny one-room apartment that was full of light without actually looking anywhere but at Elizabeth. He'd been apart from her for only a week but it had been the longest week of his life.

He cleared his throat and unbuttoned his coat.

'You're not staying,' she said sharply.

He'd been expecting this sort of welcome but still he winced. At least she'd let him into the apartment. He hadn't been sure she would even do that.

'I have something for you.' He pulled out a notebook from his inside pocket, where he'd kept it to keep dry. 'You left this behind.'

She stared at it with wide eyes. 'You came all this way to give me that?'

'No. I would have come anyway. It just might have taken me a bit longer.'

Her jaw clenched. She wasn't going to make this easy for him. He didn't blame her a bit.

'Look, Elizabeth, I've been standing outside your apartment for over an hour. I'm freezing. Do you have coffee?'

There was a definite flicker but she remained stony. 'I'm a New Yorker. Of course I have coffee.' And then she closed her eyes and sighed. 'Okay. I'll make you one. And then you can go.'

This was much more than he'd hoped for. 'Thank you.'

She shrugged her coat and woolly hat off and hung them in a store cupboard by the door. 'Whatever.'

The kitchen was at the far end of the open-plan living space. Knowing she wouldn't invite him to sit, he took a stool at the breakfast bar that separated the kitchen from the tiny dining area.

'I read through your notebook,' he said while she fixed the coffee, her back to him.

She stiffened a touch then opened a cupboard to remove two mugs.

'You're writing a script.'

Not a flicker of response this time.

'Second chance love.' He rubbed his jaw. 'Not about us. Not exactly. I could figure that for myself. But still, second chance love. The path to redemption and forgiveness.'

There was a long period of silence, then, her back still to him, she opened the cupboard under the sink and pulled out some kitchen roll. She blew her nose.

'Elizabeth?'

'Can you please go?' There was nothing stony about her voice now. It trembled and choked as she added, 'There's a coffee shop across the road. Please. Go. I can't see you right now.'

'Elizabeth...'

'Please?' Then she turned to face him. Tears fell down her cheeks in a torrent. 'Please, Xander, just get out. I can't bear it.'

He was off the stool and hauling her into his arms before he could blink.

Smoothing her hair with his hand, he held her tightly. 'Elizabeth, please, don't cry. Punch me or kick me, anything you like, just don't cry like this. I'm not worth it.'

She punched a fist against his chest. 'I know you're not.'

'I'm a selfish, selfish man.'

'Yes.'

'I put the business above everything else.'

She punched him again while still sobbing into the crook of his neck. 'Yes.'

'I walked away from you once because I was scared.'

She stilled.

'And then I let you walk away from me because I was terrified.'

He took hold of the hand he feared was about to thump him again and held it tight against his heart. 'You were the best person I had ever known. I fell in love with you the minute I saw you and I have never stopped loving you. I've done everything in my power to forget you but you've been living in my heart for so long you've claimed squatters' rights.'

She made a noise like a choking hyena.

He smiled and kissed her hair reverently. 'Those plans we made ten years ago, I meant every word of them. I wanted to spend the rest of my life with you and have our four babies. Samuel, Giannis, Imogen and Rebecca.'

She wriggled enough to tilt her head back and look at him with puffy eyes. 'You remember?' she whispered.

'Always.' He couldn't hold her tightly enough. What a fool he'd been. 'But you're right. I should have fought for you.'

He closed his eyes. 'I should have fought for you,' he repeated. 'I didn't. I thought I was doing the right thing. And maybe you're right that the business meant more to me than you but I didn't see it like that. The family business was my life. It was who I was. It didn't cross my mind that I could walk away from it. All I knew for certain was that I didn't want you within a thousand miles of my world. The one good person I knew from it was Ana and all I could think was if she couldn't cope with our world—and she'd been raised in it—then how could you? You wouldn't have, not then. And at her funeral I knew I'd made the right choice to leave you behind because it cut me to pieces to see her coffin lowered into the ground. If anything had happened to you it would have killed me.'

Elizabeth's eyes shone with tears but she kept them on his face, not interrupting, letting him spill his guts.

'Yanis and Katerina are going to divorce.'

'Really?' she whispered hoarsely.

'*Nai*. It is time. Yanis will have custody of Loukas but between us we'll make sure he spends lots of time with her. If and when she's better they'll look at it again but to keep Loukas settled they've agreed this is the way forward.'

She gave a tentative smile. 'What brought it on?'

'You.'

'Me?'

He nodded. 'You were right about that as well. They'd stayed together to protect the business. You made me see that my family have used the damned business as a means of controlling each other for too long. I bear guilt for that too, but it stops now. It's us, the people in the family, the people we love who matter. Yanis and Katerina will never find happiness together but I hope they will find happiness with other lovers in the future, and I hope the cycle of revenge stops now too. You said a long time ago that no one knew what was in Ana's head when she got behind the wheel. Ana made that choice and I need to let it go; the blame, the guilt, all of it, but I don't know if I can do it without you.'

He paused for breath and rubbed his thumbs across her cheekbones. 'When I read through your notebook and pieced together what your story-line would be about, that's when it struck me that you'd opened your heart again enough to be able to write about love, and if you, someone who has been through far more than me, can open your heart and take that leap of faith... I have done some stupid things in my life but denying my love for you last week was the stupidest of them all. I do love you, Elizabeth. When I walked away from you ten years ago I had to put my heart in a vice to get through it. Having you back broke it free and I didn't even realise. This past week...it's felt like all my limbs have been ripped off. I can't be without you. Please, come back to me, I beg you. I know I don't deserve a third chance but I'm lost without you and I swear on Loukas's life I will never put anyone or anything above you again, not even my own fears or pride.'

For the longest time, Elizabeth didn't say anything. And then she gave a tentative smile. 'Wow. That was some speech.'

He gave a shaky laugh. 'I've been going over and over what I was going to say to you since I left Diadonus. So what do you say? Will you give me another chance? Will you take the leap of faith with me?' He knew she loved him but was it enough for her to forgive him?

Her smile widened and she looped her arms around his neck and raised herself onto her toes to press a kiss to his mouth. 'I'll think about it.'

'Take all the time you need.'

She rubbed her nose against his. 'If you reject me again I will cut your heart out.'

'Cut it out now. It's yours. It's yours for ever.'

Now she put her lips back to his and kissed him with such sweet passion his heart soared.

'I've thought about it,' she said when they came up for air, 'and the answer is yes. You're my world. I can function without you but it's only when I'm with you that I feel whole. I don't want to be without you.'

And then her soft lips were on his again and he knew they would be the lips he kissed for the rest of his life.

EPILOGUE

ELIZABETH COULDN'T STOP SMILING. Her mouth had been curved up for so long her cheeks ached in protest. It made not a jot of difference. This was the happiest day of her life and the best bit was about to happen.

Xander solemnly took the simple gold band from Loukas and then, a grin widening on his own face, slid it onto her finger.

She would never take it off.

Then it was her turn to slide Xander's wedding ring onto his finger.

She knew in her heart he would never take it off.

The renewal of their vows done, they turned to face the congregation, who all stood in applause.

The church was jam-packed. Having done a beachside quickie marriage the first time with only two of the hotel's bar staff as witnesses, this time they'd wanted to do it properly and exchange their vows in front of everyone they knew.

They'd chosen to do it *all* properly. Elizabeth wore a traditional white floor-length dress with a train

Loukas kept hiding under, Xander was gorgeous in a black tux.

Her hand clasped tightly in his, she scanned the congregation. There was Katerina, still jaundiced but hopeful of recovery. After a horrendous relapse on the day she'd been discharged, she'd frightened herself enough to finally admit that she was an alcoholic. She'd been dry for two months and in another four would qualify for a liver transplant. All Elizabeth could do was pray she stayed dry.

In a surprise twist, Katerina and Yanis had decided to give their marriage another chance. Somewhere in all the years of pain and substance abuse, love had grown. It had taken them both getting sober to realise it.

In the front row to the left were Xander's parents, both pretending to be delighted at this renewal of vows. A declaration of peace had been issued and so far all parties were sticking to it. Elizabeth didn't believe for a minute that it would last.

Next to Mirela and Dragan sat Elizabeth's father and stepmother, who had taken one look at her mother sitting in the front row to the right, and changed pews. Elizabeth was very much looking forward to seeing how her mother and Mirela got on during the reception. Xander had started a sweepstake over which mother-in-law would 'accidentally' spill something on the other first.

She couldn't resist waving at Piper Mancini, bouncing her bonny newborn baby and looking utterly beautiful beside her handsome, protective husband Dante. Directly behind them sat Zayn and Amalia, pressed close together. Beside them were Benjamin and Julianna Carter. Rumours abounded that both Amalia and Julianna were pregnant and Elizabeth was determined to get them alone later to see if the rumours were true and share her own news—that the pregnancy test she'd taken a fortnight ago had been positive.

There was Yanis, now six months free from drugs and looking healthier by the day. There was Loukas, their ring-bearer, a happy soul unrecognisable from the scared child she'd met six months ago.

And then she turned her head to see the most important one of all. Xander. Her love, her rock, her best friend. And soon they would be parents, something that had made him spray champagne all over her to celebrate with.

As he leaned his head down to kiss her, she knew she would never regret taking this leap of faith.

* * * * *

If you enjoyed this
BRIDES FOR BILLIONAIRES *story,*
don't forget to read the
first three instalments

MARRIED FOR THE TYCOON'S EMPIRE
by Abby Green
MARRIED FOR THE ITALIAN'S HEIR
by Rachael Thomas
MARRIED FOR THE SHEIKH'S DUTY
by Tara Pammi

Available now!

#3501 BRIDE BY ROYAL DECREE
Wedlocked!
by Caitlin Crews
King Reza's betrothed, Princess Magdalena, disappeared years ago. But a mysterious photograph brings them together again. Fiercely independent Maggy won't accept her birthright on any terms but her own—so Reza will have to use sensual persuasions that Maggy will be helpless to resist!

#3502 THE SHEIKH'S SECRET SON
Secret Heirs of Billionaires
by Maggie Cox
Sheikh Zafir el-Kalil will do anything to secure his child—even marry the woman who kept their son a secret! But Darcy Carrick is older and wiser now, and it will take more than soft words and sweet seduction to win back her love...

#3503 ACQUIRED BY HER GREEK BOSS
by Chantelle Shaw
Greek tycoon Alekos Gionakis thinks he knows his secretary, until he's forced to reappraise his most precious asset! Alekos offers beautiful Sara Lovejoy a meeting with her unknown family, provided she agrees to become his mistress. But Sara's innocence is priceless...

#3504 VOWS THEY CAN'T ESCAPE
by Heidi Rice
Xanthe Carmichael has discovered two things: that she's *still* married, and her husband could take half her business! Xanthe is hit by lust when she confronts him with divorce papers...but will Dane begin stirring the smoldering embers of their passion?

YOU CAN FIND MORE INFORMATION ON UPCOMING HARLEQUIN® TITLES, FREE EXCERPTS AND MORE AT WWW.HARLEQUIN.COM.

HPCNM0117RB

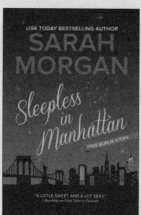

*Even unsentimental Alessandro Di Sione can't deny his
grandfather's dream of retrieving a scandalous painting.
Yet its return depends on outspoken Princess Gabriella.
While traveling together to locate the painting, Gabby
is drawn to this guilt-ridden man. Could their passion
be his salvation?*

Read on for a sneak preview of
THE LAST DI SIONE CLAIMS HIS PRIZE
*the final part in the unmissable new eight-book
Harlequin Presents® series*
THE BILLIONAIRE'S LEGACY

Alessandro was so different than she was. Gabby had
never truly fully appreciated just how different men and
women were. In a million ways, big and small.

Yes, there was the obvious, but it was more than that.
And it was those differences that suddenly caused her to
glory in who she was, what she was. To feel, if only for
a moment, that she completely understood herself both
body and soul, and that they were united in one desire.

"Kiss me, Princess," he said, his voice low, strained.

He was affected.

So she had won.

She had been the one to make him burn.

But she'd made a mistake if she'd thought this game
had one winner and one loser. She was right down there
with him. And she didn't care about winning anymore.

She couldn't deny him, not now. Not when he was

looking at her like she was a woman and not a girl, or an owl. Not when he was looking at her like she was the sun, moon and all the stars combined. Bright, brilliant and something that held the power to hold him transfixed.

Something more than what she was. Because Gabriella D'Oro had never transfixed anyone. Not her parents. Not a man.

But he was looking at her like she mattered. She didn't feel like shrinking into a wall or melting into the scenery. She wanted him to keep looking.

She didn't want to hide from this. She wanted all of it.

Slowly, so slowly, so that she could savor the feel of him, relish the sensations of his body beneath her touch, she slid her hand up his throat, feeling the heat of his skin, the faint scratch of whiskers.

Then she moved to cup his jaw, his cheek.

"I've never touched a man like this before," she confessed.

And she wasn't even embarrassed by the confession, because he was still looking at her like he wanted her.

He moved closer, covering her hand with his. She could feel his heart pounding heavily, could sense the tension running through his frame. "I've touched a great many women," he said, his tone grave. "But at the moment it doesn't seem to matter."

That was when she kissed him.

Don't miss
THE LAST DI SIONE CLAIMS HIS PRIZE,
available February 2017 wherever
Harlequin Presents® books and ebooks are sold.

www.Harlequin.com

HARLEQUIN
Presents®

**Don't miss Heidi Rice's thrilling
Harlequin Presents debut—a story of
a couple tempestuously reunited!**

Xanthe Carmichael has just discovered two things:
1. Her ex-husband could take half her business
2. She's actually still married to him!

When she jets off to New York, divorce papers in hand, Xanthe
is prepared for the billionaire bad boy's slick offices…but not for
the spear of lust that hits her the moment she sees Dane Redmond
again! Has her body no shame, no recollection of the pain he
caused? But Dane is stalling… Is he really checking the fine print
or planning to stir the smoldering embers of their passion and
tempt her back into the marriage bed?

Don't miss

VOWS THEY
CAN'T ESCAPE

Available February 2017

I ♥ &Harlequin Presents

JUST CAN'T GET ENOUGH
OF THE ALPHA MALE?
Us either!

Come join us at **I Heart Presents** to hear the latest from your favorite Harlequin Presents authors and get special behind-the-scenes secrets of the Presents team!

With access to the latest breaking news and special promotions, **I Heart Presents** is *the* destination for all things Presents. Get up close and personal with the sexy alpha heroes who make your heart beat faster and share your love of these glitzy, glamorous reads with the authors, the editors and fellow Presents fans!